BACK TO PLYMOUTH

LOVE THROUGHOUT TIME

BOOK EIGHT

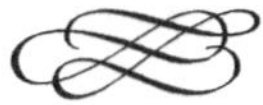

ID JOHNSON

For Dee Dee

CONTENTS

TRADITION DEMANDS SACRIFICE

Alyssa

When I hear three short raps on my apartment door, I know it's my best friend Danielle. "Come on, Alyssa," she calls. "We're going to be late!"

I swing the door open, my half-laced bodice hanging loose and my stockings bunched at my ankles. Danielle grins at the sight of me, already put together in her neat black gown and white cap. Somehow, she makes seventeenth-century Puritan modesty look natural.

"I had to wrangle this thing into place," I mutter, tugging at my clothes. "I swear these reenactment costumes are some kind of punishment."

She laughs and sweeps past me into the apartment, carrying a box that smells suspiciously of maple donuts. "Consider it penance for living in the birthplace of Thanksgiving. Tradition demands sacrifice."

I roll my eyes, but I can't help smiling. Danielle has a way of making even the most awkward situations, like dressing up as pilgrims for a festival, feel like an adventure.

She fastens the ties at the back of my bodice while I check that the basket of dried corn husks is ready for the crafts station. My classroom's contribution to the festival is "Pilgrim Life," complete with candlemaking and storytelling. Danielle's sixth graders will be reading aloud passages from William Bradford, which she insists will hold their attention better than a video.

"Your hat," she says, plopping the stiff white coif onto my head. "You'd forget it every year if I didn't force it on you."

"Because it's ridiculous." I catch my reflection in the mirror by the door and grimace. Between the flat linen cap and the plain wool dress, I look less like a pilgrim and more like someone who lost a bet.

"Authenticity, Alyssa. Embrace it."

I groan and let her shepherd me out the door. We load baskets of apples for bobbing, the carefully folded costumes for our students, stacks of paper plates, and napkins decorated with turkeys into the trunk of my car. I grab my coffee on the last trip, and Danielle tucks the box of donuts behind us in the back seat, a secret stash for us when the chaos of the festival becomes too much.

"Did we forget anything?" I ask.

"Probably. We usually do," she says with a grin as she slides into the passenger seat.

"We'll remember it about ten minutes after we get started—whatever it is," I say as I jump in behind the wheel and fire it up.

The road curves along the line of trees, their fallen leaves tumbling in the wind like embers from a fire. I keep one hand steady on the wheel and the other wrapped around my coffee, and the hum of the engine fills the quiet between us.

Danielle leans against the window, her cap slipping just a little to one side. She's been my closest friend since childhood, growing up more in my house than her own. My parents treated her like another daughter, taking her to church with us every Sunday, pulling up a chair for her at every holiday table. Summers meant long stretches at my grandparents' place, where she and I spent evenings chasing fireflies or sneaking extra pie from Grandma's kitchen. She's the kind of person I don't need to fill silence with, but she breaks it first.

"Will your family be at the festival today?" she asks.

I nod, my eyes still on the road. "Yeah, of course. They always come. My parents like helping out with the kids. Mom usually ends up at the food station, and Dad wrangles stragglers between tents. James and Chloe will be there, too. You know how James complains every year, but he'll still show up. And Chloe loves any excuse to wear a costume."

I smile just thinking about them, but when I glance sideways at Danielle, I see sadness in her eyes. She covers it quickly, turning her gaze back to the blur of orange and red leaves outside.

Her voice is light when she answers. "Sounds like a full Montgomery turnout, then."

It's supposed to be a joke, but it doesn't land. I know her too well. I see the shadow beneath the words. Her family won't be there. They never are.

I grip the steering wheel a little tighter. "They're looking forward to seeing you, too," I say quickly. "Chloe still talks about that diary story you told last year, the one about the girl hiding her writing in her apron. She swears it made her want to start journaling again."

Danielle gives a soft laugh, but her eyes stay on the window. "Your sister's too sweet."

"You know it's not just her," I press. "You've got a way with people. Not just the kids, my parents love you, too."

Her smile shifts, warmer now, but quieter. "Thanks. It's just that sometimes it'd be nice to have my own people cheering me on, not just yours."

The words are so soft I almost miss them over the hum of the car. My chest tightens. I reach across the console and squeeze her hand.

"You've got me," I say.

She squeezes back, and the sadness in her eyes eases, just a little.

We let the silence take over again, but this time it feels easier. The road straightens, opening to a glimpse of water ahead. The ocean shines steel-blue under the morning sun, and as we crest the hill, the harbor comes into view, with banners strung along the streets, families already milling toward the tents, the replica Mayflower rising against the sky.

I exhale slowly, a strange flutter starting low in my stomach. Every year, the festival feels the same, but this time, something is different, though I can't quite pinpoint what it is that's been making me feel this way.

We approach the beach road, the ocean stretching wide on either side. The sun is in just the right position to turn the water on my left into shards of glass, reflecting light that makes me squint. Danielle is talking about how she wants to get her kids to actually read William Bradford without falling asleep, her voice as animated as her hand gestures. She's always been so good at storytelling and improvising with the children.

I'm half-listening, half-focusing on the traffic ahead. Then, out of nowhere, movement flashes at the edge of the road.

A deer bolts across the road from nowhere, its body a blur of brown and white. I gasp, and it leaps straight across the asphalt, so close I can see the whites of its eyes.

"Hold on!" I shout, jerking the wheel hard to the right.

The tires shriek against the pavement. Danielle yelps, grabbing the dash. The world tilts violently. Metal shudders. Glass rattles. For a split second, I think we're clear, seeing the deer bounding away in my rearview mirror, but the swerve is too sharp. The car skids sideways, and the guardrail rushes up faster than I can correct.

Then we're through it.

The road drops away beneath us, and I can't stop the car from sliding across the wet sand. The scream tears from my throat, with wind roaring in my ears as the ocean surges closer and closer.

The impact slams through my body.

The front end hits the water like a hammer blow. My seatbelt bites into my chest, my teeth jarring, and icy spray explodes across the windshield. For one dizzy second, I think maybe we'll stop, maybe the car will float, but the nose dips lower, dragging us forward, and water surges up the hood.

Cold water seeps in instantly, rushing around my ankles. My

fingers scramble at the wheel, useless. Danielle claw at her seatbelt, her face pale and her mouth open in shock. The car groans as it tips deeper.

"Danielle!" I scream, panic shooting through my chest.

I slam my fists against the car door, fumbling with the buckle to my seatbelt, but everything is too slippery. The ocean pours in faster now, rising past our knees, climbing to our waists.

I turn my head, water stinging my eyes, and call again, louder, my voice raw. "Danielle!"

She doesn't answer. She must be in shock.

Finally, my buckle clicks, and I wrench the seatbelt free. Cold water slams into my chest, stealing my breath for a second, but I don't hesitate. I reach across to Danielle, unbuckling her seatbelt just as desperately.

Her hands flail, gripping the strap, and I yank it with every ounce of strength I have. Another click and she's free, too, slumping against me for a second before I shove her toward the door. The car tilts even more, and water pours in faster, filling the cabin like someone pouring a glass of water from beneath us..

I shove with all I have, kicking my legs against the seat and the dashboard, finally forcing the door open. Freezing water crashes in, dragging us both sideways. I grab Danielle's arm and kick hard, trying to push us up, toward the surface, toward air.

I guide her, my grip tight, urging her up, splashing, gasping. My lungs burn, and my chest aches, but I keep pulling, keep kicking, pushing, and fighting.

A blur of light above cuts through the darkness, a thin promise. I can see the surface.

Panic and determination mix and drag us upward, toward the air that feels impossibly far, impossibly necessary.

When we break the surface, I gasp, my lungs screaming for air. Danielle's eyes are closed, but as I lift her above the water, she draws in a sharp, shivering breath. Relief hits me for a heartbeat, and then a massive wave crashes over us, dragging us down again.

The cold water swallows the last breath from my lips, and the world dissolves into silence.

MAIDENS

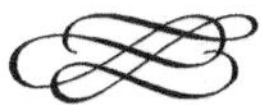

Isaac

THE WIND CARRIES A BITTER COLD BITE OFF THE OCEAN, CUTTING through the layers of wool I wear. I tighten my cloak around my shoulders, glancing down at the shoreline. Henry trudges beside me, his boots sinking into the wet sand with every step.

"Looks calmer than this morning," he mutters, squinting toward the horizon.

"Don't trust it. The sea can turn quick," I reply, keeping my eyes on the wooden stakes marking the small harbor. The settlement is still young, its houses rough and small. Waves lap and churn against the sand, restless, carrying driftwood and foam, and I can feel the ocean's power here, so close to shore.

Henry slows, pausing mid-step, his head tilting sharply toward the surf. I follow his gaze. He freezes, his finger pointing toward the water. "Look! Over there!"

I see two figures struggling in the surf, tiny against the swell, their flailing arms and heads bobbing as the waves claw at them. My heart leaps into my throat. "By God!" I shout. Without another thought, I sprint toward them, with Henry right behind me.

The tide grabs at my ankles, dragging, slowing me, but I push forward. I keep my eyes on them, frantic and floundering.

Henry reaches my side, shouting, "Stay with us! We'll get you out!"

I dive headfirst into the cold water, and each stroke is a battle against the pull of the surf. The first woman's hair sticks to her face, her mouth opening and closing as she gasps. Panic spikes in me as I grab her under the arms, holding her head above the waves, my legs kicking fiercely to fight the tide.

"I've got you! Keep your head above water!" I shout over the roar of the ocean when I resurface to take a breath.

Henry grips the second woman under the arms. "Easy now, the Lord hath spared you!" he calls, kicking hard, keeping both of them afloat as he guides her toward the shore.

We push through the current, the water relentlessly trying to sink us. My lungs burn and my chest aches, but I refuse to stop, and I won't let go. Finally, we scrape onto the sand, collapsing, coughing and sputtering, soaked to the bone.

We lie there for a moment, our hearts hammering, catching our breath. The women stare at us, coughing and trembling, ghostly pale from the cold and fear, yet alive.

I straighten, water dripping from my clothes. When I finally catch my breath, I speak. "Are you well? Did you swallow too much water?'

The ladies cough, looking around us for a moment. One of them asks, "Who are you?"

Though I'm confused as to why she would ask such a question at the moment, I reply, "My name is Isaac Owens, and this is Henry Lewis." I nod toward my friend.

The first woman blinks at me, her eyebrows nearly touching as she mirrors my own confusion. "I'm... Alyssa," she says, still trembling. "Uh, Alyssa Montgomery. And this is—" She glances at her companion.

"Danielle Whitman," the other woman finishes quietly, her eyes wide and wary.

Henry leans forward, rubbing his hands together. "What transpired? How did you come to be in the sea?"

Alyssa swallows hard, her hands shaking. "The waves... were enormous. We tried to hold on, but the water... dragged us under. Where are we?"

"You're near Plymouth." I say. "A quaint village named after the city in England we sailed from. I take it you are not from here?" Where could they have come from? I do not see a ship nearby.

"We're still in Plymouth?" Alyssa asks. "Where is everyone? Where are all the other reenactors and teachers?"

"Reenactors?" I ask. "I'm not familiar with the term."

Danielle looks around, slowly standing and sputtering. "If I may ask, how long has it been since you set sail from Plymouth, England?"

"Nearly a full year ago," I reply.

The women exchange a glance, and for a second, I believe I see a glimmer of fear in each of their eyes, which puzzles me. We just saved them. We certainly mean them no harm.

Danielle looks up at me and then Henry. "We were aboard a ship from Bristol, England," she says, her voice trembling. "We were bound for a settlement further south when the wind picked up and carried us north."

Henry and I share a worried look. It's not uncommon for ships to get lost in these waters, but to survive a wreck is another thing entirely. Their party may not have made it.

"You're safe now," I tell them. "We'll get you to our settlement. You'll be dry and fed."

The women look at one another nervously again, and I can feel the apprehension in them. They're disoriented and unsure of where they are.

"Can you walk?" Henry asks gently, holding out a hand to Danielle.

She hesitates, then takes it, leaning on him. Alyssa does the same with me, her icy fingers curling around my wrist.

We move slowly along the sand toward the village. Men pass us carrying barrels and sacks full of supplies with determination. The lean stores of food are a stark reminder of the colony's struggles. Hunger and sickness have left their mark. I feel the tug of responsibility, that familiar ache in my chest. We must help preserve this fragile settlement.

I look at Alyssa, who scans her surroundings like a deer in an open meadow. "You say you're from Bristol?" I ask. "Your manner of speaking is quite peculiar."

Alyssa bites her lip. "We came from Bristol, but we grew up in several different places. France, Hispania, even the far east for a while. That has made our accents a bit muddled."

Henry glances at me then back at the two young women. "We'll get you warm first, then find you something to eat. You've been through enough today."

I nod toward one of the homes. "The Tinkers will take you in," I say. "They have room, and they'll see you warm and fed."

Alyssa blinks at me, her lips parted, shivering. "Thank you," she whispers.

The front door of the Tinker house is open and smoke curls from the chimney. Thomas Tinker and his wife step out, recognition in their eyes as they spot us. "Owens? Lewis?" Mr. Tinker calls, his voice carrying over the wind. "What's happened?"

"The storm this morning at sea," I reply, guiding Alyssa gently. "These two women were caught in it and shipwrecked. We brought them in."

The Tinkers' eyes fill with dismay as they take in the drenched, shivering women. "Come in, quickly!" Mrs. Tinker urges, stepping aside to let us pass. The warmth of the hearth hits me as soon as we enter, carrying the smell of soup and baking bread.

Mrs. Tinker ushers the women through the low doorway into a smaller, warmer room. "Quickly now. You'll catch your death if you stay in those wet clothes," she scolds gently.

Henry and I wait near the hearth, listening to the soft rustle of fabric from the other room.

When the women emerge, shivering slightly but more composed

in dry garments, Mrs. Tinker ladles broth into bowls and sets one before each of them. "Here, something to warm you," she says. The women take it with tentative hands, sipping carefully, their eyes still wide and scanning the room. Mrs. Tinker returns to gather their wet garments and lay them by the hearth to dry.

I glance around the Tinker house. Supplies are sparse, carefully measured. Every surface holds only the necessities: lean stores of flour, a few dried herbs, a modest stash of salted meat.

I step forward, clearing my throat. "These are Mistress Montgomery and Mistress Whitman," I say, gesturing to the women. Their eyes widen at hearing their names spoken aloud, almost as if they're hearing it themselves for the first time.

Mrs. Tinker leans closer, smiling gently. "Well, maidens, you'll be safe here for the night," she says, her voice warm and soothing.

The women murmur their thanks, their voices low and cautious, as if testing the sound of the words in their new surroundings.

Henry claps me on the shoulder. "We best get ourselves out of these wet clothes before we freeze alongside them," he mutters.

I nod, the chill from the surf still clinging to me. I excuse myself, offering a small bow to Mrs. Tinker. "We'll return to check on all of you shortly," I say, and with that, Henry and I part ways, each heading toward our respective home to change clothing and dry off. The wet wool chafes at my skin, and the memory of the surf still bites at my lungs, but my thoughts are already tangled with the women.

It's quite strange that two women who have lived in far-off lands, France and España, India and England, could be washed up on this lonely shore, disoriented and shivering, yet still carrying themselves with a graceful dignity and strength. The way they speak, peculiar and unfamiliar, sticks in my mind.

I tug off the damp outer layers, wishing the warmth of a fire for myself, and the oddest sense of anticipation prickles in my chest. Who are they? What manner of lives have they led to bring them here, to Plymouth, at this moment?

They'll be taken care of here, for now, yes, but I'm already planning how to keep watch over them. For though they are strangers, there is something in them, something I don't fully grasp, that tells me their presence here is no ordinary happenstance.

THE EASY PART

Alyssa

MY FINGERS ACHE AROUND THE ROUGH HANDLE OF THE LOG BASKET, splinters snagging my skin as I carry it across the yard behind Danielle. The Tinker family's cottage crouches against the edge of the clearing, smoke billowing from the chimney. Mr. and Mrs. Tinker are already busy stacking firewood by the door, and their son Samuel, who can't be more than fourteen, is chopping steadily, each swing echoing like a heartbeat through the crisp, cool air.

Danielle walks just ahead of me, her skirts brushing against her ankles, her breath clouding in the cold. She always looks composed, but here, dressed in borrowed linen and wool, she looks like she belongs. Me? I feel like a child on a field trip who lost her group.

When Thomas, Mr. Tinker, carries another armload inside and his wife, Jane, disappears through the doorway too, Danielle pauses at the edge of the woodpile, the smallest grin tugging at her lips. It's the first time we've been alone since we washed up here hours ago.

I drop the basket with a thud and whisper, "Okay, I have to ask. How in the world did you come up with that story? Bristol? Heading south? Like you had it loaded and ready. And the accent thing? Genius."

She laughs softly, brushing her dark hair back under her cap. "When I realized where we were... or *when* we *are*, rather, well, you know me. I've always been good at improv. It's a classroom survival skill. Half the time, I don't know what I'm going to say until it's out of my mouth."

"Yeah, but usually that's with sixth graders asking if Helen Keller was a real person or if you'd marry Abe Lincoln." I glance at the cottage windows, lowering my voice further. "Not with seventeenth-century settlers deciding whether or not we belong in the nuthouse or if we should be burned at the stake."

Danielle's grin fades, but her eyes stay steady. "I know, but it worked, didn't it? They bought it—for now."

I rub my hands together, more to steady my nerves than for warmth. The silence between us stretches heavy before I finally let the question slip. "So... we really did that, then? We actually fell back in time to the 1620s."

Danielle doesn't hesitate. She nods, scanning the forest as if the answer is carved in a tree there. "Yep. We sure did."

My chest tightens. I was hoping she'd say no, that there was some rational explanation, but Danielle never lies to me. And what else could it possibly be?

I let out a shaky laugh. "Great. Just great. Two teachers from 2025, no phones, no coffee, no indoor plumbing... and about four hundred years off schedule."

"At least we landed together," she says, pulling me in for a hug.

"I thought I'd lost you for a second, and it was the scariest second of my life," I admit.

By the time Mrs. Tinker returns, thanking us for the help, we're working side by side again, our hands red from the cold, our skirts dusty from the wood. I can't stop thinking of my parents, my brother and sister, James and Chloe, imagining them at home, waiting for the authorities to bring news, terrified that they will hear our bodies were never recovered. The thought twists my stomach.

Whatever this is—a dream, a nightmare, history magically brought to life—tonight, when the Tinkers offer us a place to stay, I know we will say yes. There is nowhere else to go.

The warmth of the Tinkers' hearth and the small comfort of familiarity in this strange century feel like the only things keeping me from freezing entirely.

THE SUNRISE SLANTS LOW, ORANGE AND CRIMSON, WHEN MRS. TINKER nudges us awake. My back aches from the straw mattress, my neck stiff from tossing and turning all night, but I force myself up. Danielle is already sitting, her cap slightly askew, her hair sticking out like she never slept either.

"Come, maidens," Mrs. Tinker says gently. "There is enough work for all of us."

Work. The word carries weight here. If we're going to stay, we can't just sit by the fire and take up space.

Outside, the air bites sharper than yesterday, and the dew still clings to the edges of the garden rows. Danielle takes the empty bucket from Mrs. Tinker, and I follow her down toward the well.

The rope burns my hands as we lower it, the creak of wood echoing. The water is dark and cold when it splashes up, heavy enough that I stumble before finding my grip. Danielle steadies me with a wry smile.

"Guess all those gym sessions didn't prepare us for seventeenth-century weight training," she mutters.

I laugh under my breath, though my arms are already trembling.

Back nearer the cottage, Mrs. Tinker sets us to work pulling the last of the carrots from the garden, our skirts dragging through the dirt. The soil is cold, and the morning chill seeps through our layers. My hands ache. My fingers are numb. I realize how exposed we are in this century. The work is steady, unrelenting, and utterly foreign.

Danielle leans close. "Do you think we can figure out a way back?" she whispers.

"I don't know," I reply, keeping my voice low. "I keep trying to imagine how my parents must feel, waiting for news, thinking we went down with the car in the ocean."

Her jaw tightens. "I know. I thought of that, too, and it made me feel sick. Well, at least my folks won't be pacing the floors. My family doesn't care that much."

I glance at her, biting back a shiver from more than the cold. "I'm sorry, Danielle. I hate that your parents are too wrapped up in their own bullshit to notice how amazing and beautiful you are. And my parents are certainly just as devastated over losing you as they are me," I say, squeezing her hand.

She gives me a small smile and shrugs. "Well, I guess we just have to survive today and hope we can find a way home to your family."

I nod, staring at the meager garden. When we finally have a bundle of carrots set aside, Mrs. Tinker steps closer, brushing her hands on her apron. "There's a gathering this afternoon," she tells us. "We should start heading that way. Governor Bradford will speak, and Captain Standish, too. You are welcome to come along."

I swallow hard. A meeting, in the heart of the settlement, with everyone gathered? Danielle falls in step beside me. "Are you nervous to meet Bradford?" I ask.

"Of course. I was just writing notecards about him, and now we'll be face to face. What if he isn't so welcoming after all?"

THE MEETING HOUSE RISES BEFORE US, ITS TIMBER WALLS ROUGH BUT solid. Thomas pushes the heavy door open, and we step inside. The warmth hits immediately, along with the low murmur of settlers. The wooden benches are mostly full, and the smell of wood, wool, and body odor clings to everything.

At the front, a man stands reading from a sheet of paper, his voice steady and calm, though the occupants of the room listen with careful attention. He looks up as we enter.

Mr. Tinker leans close to us. "That's Governor Bradford," he whispers. "Our leader."

I watch as he addresses the settlers, speaking about rations and food storage, and how each family must measure carefully and save enough for the winter. It's exactly what I expected. Teaching Plymouth's history all these years, I've known how precarious life was here, how hunger was always a shadow over the colony. Seeing it unfold before me, though, makes it immediate, tangible. Perhaps I was brought back to this moment to do more than observe, to offer whatever small knowledge and skills Danielle and I can contribute to help them survive.

The speech winds down, and settlers begin to mingle, exchanging quiet words and checking stores. Governor Bradford walks toward us, a tall, broad-shouldered man at his side. Bradford offers a polite smile. "I am William Bradford, governor of this settlement," he says.

The man beside him inclines his head. "Captain Standish, at your service," he says, removing his hat and placing it over his heart.

Bradford looks at us and adds with a jovial tone, "I understand you've recently arrived in Plymouth. Welcome."

I force myself to remain stoic. "Thank you. I am Alyssa Montgomery," I say. "And this is Danielle Whitman. The Tinkers have been kind enough to take us in after our ship went down."

Standish, who is stockier, with sharp eyes, folds his arms. "Aye. Henry Lewis told us. And where do you say you're from?"

I glance at Danielle, but I don't hesitate. "Bristol, England," I say. "We were bound for a settlement further south. A storm carried us off course."

Standish narrows his eyes, studying me like he's measuring my worth. "Aye. We witnessed that storm blow in. You're blessed to be alive."

Danielle smiles, adding, "We feel very fortunate. Thank you kindly, sir."

Bradford's gaze lingers a moment on Danielle's face, then he looks back at me. "You're both welcome here as long as you need."

"Thank you, Governor Bradford," I tell him. "We will certainly earn our keep."

"It was a pleasure to meet you both," Bradford says.

Standish straightens, tipping his hat once more. "Indeed. I trust you will find your place here."

They move off toward other settlers, and with their attention gone, the room feels less charged. I shift my gaze across the room, where Isaac leans against a pillar, his arms crossed loosely. Henry stands nearby, his eyes moving briefly to Danielle, who straightens under his glance before turning back to me, a rosy blush blooming across her cheeks.

I nudge her ribs with my elbow and wink. "Girl, please do not fall for the handsome man who's four hundred years older than you," I whisper.

She laughs softly, and I grin, shaking my head. The meeting wraps up, and we join the stream of settlers filing out of the meeting house.

Danielle mutters sarcastically, "Well, that wasn't terrifying at all."

I laugh, tugging my shawl tighter. "I hope that wasn't the easy part."

"If that was the easy part, then I don't even want to stick around for the hard part."

"Seems like you were causing some *hard parts* on your own," I reply, causing Danielle to burst into laughter, a most welcome sound in such a dark and cold place.

"Behave, or we'll be punished for giggling like we were every day of junior high," is her response after catching her breath.

As we trudge along the rough path back to the Tinker house, I can't help but notice the children of the village, their pale faces, dry lips, and a deep chest cough that rattles their small frames.

"They're all so sick," I murmur to Danielle. "See their gums? The bruising?"

She leans closer to me, frowning. "Scurvy," she whispers. "They've been missing fresh fruit for months."

Mrs. Tinker overhears this part of our conversation and nods toward one of the families. "The Connors," she says quietly, "have been struggling these last weeks."

I gather every ounce of courage I have and approach the parents. "Sir, ma'am, your children are suffering from an illness that I have experienced. There are plants that could help them get stronger."

Danielle is right beside me. "Pine needle tea, spruce tips boiled in water, fresh berries if you can find them, dandelion leaves, chickweed, even small roots. Boil them into a broth or tea, and give them several cups full each day. Cabbage, sorrel, even a few wild greens will help as well." She says it with the same certainty she had as a teenager when Grandpa taught us both how to spot edible greens on summer hikes. Back then, it was just survival practice in the woods behind his house. Now, it might actually save lives.

The mother's eyes brim with tears. "Pine needles? Dandelion leaves? Are you certain? Those are indeed plants we could actually find nearby."

"Truly." Danielle's enthusiasm could fill any parent with hope. "All you need are some of the most common plants that we have around here. Your children will get stronger each day."

A sharp voice cuts in from behind us. "Where do you young women come from? How do you know such things?" I glance back to see a sharp-eyed woman, her arms crossed. "Are ye witches?"

Another man mutters behind her, "Leave the children to God. What need have we of your strange remedies? We eat what we eat. Leave the Connors be."

I straighten, keeping my tone firm. "We are not asking to weaken your faith, only to strengthen your children. These are simple remedies found in the woods and meadows around us. They will work if you try them."

Danielle nods beside me and turns to Mrs. Connor. "You'll see the results in no time. It's worth a try."

"Very well," Mrs. Connor says, her voice firm. "We shall do as you say."

Thomas Tinker steps forward, placing a hand on his son's shoulder. "Samuel here is strong and quick," he says. "He can help fetch what you'll need. It will be no trouble at all."

Watching Samuel dash off to gather herbs and greens, I can't help but wonder again whether this is why we were thrown back in time. Maybe we're meant to help heal this village. I press my hands together and take a deep breath.

We'll do what we can here, for these children and their families, and hope that someday, somehow, we will find our way home.

LAND OF STRANGE MARVELS

Isaac

THE SUN SLANTS LOW THROUGH THE TREES, PAINTING THE FOREST floor in golden shadows. I crouch, my bow in hand, moving silently over the leaf-strewn ground. Each snap of a twig underfoot makes my pulse leap, and I pause, listening.

I came from Plymouth, England, seeking a new life in the New World, but already the weight of it presses against me. My parents are gone, and my siblings all died of fever before they could leave childhood behind. I have no one now but the others who live in this colony.

I spot movement, small and quick, and draw the bowstring. A rabbit freezes for just a heartbeat, then I release. The shot is clean, and it falls. I whisper a quiet thanks, a prayer for sustenance, and move on. Every kill matters now. Hunger lingers in every cabin, in every pale, hollow cheek. I think of the children, of the sickly ones whose ribs are too visible, whose cries are softened by weakness. I am here to provide, to protect, and I have no time for distractions. And yet, my thoughts wander.

Alyssa and Danielle—graceful, well spoken, and hardworking. I catch myself wondering if they are blessings or dangerous.

Another rabbit darts into view. I release another arrow. Another quick, precise kill. The work steadies me, focuses me, and I think of the colony, of survival, of the long months ahead. Each day demands vigilance, each action a thread in the fragile life we cling to. No one survives on sentiment alone.

I am making my way along the edge of the Tinker garden, carrying the rabbits by the feet, when I notice the two maidens bent over the rows, their sleeves rolled up and their hands deep in the soil.

"Good afternoon," I call gently, keeping my distance. "You seem well occupied."

Danielle looks up, brushing dirt from her hands, and smiles. "We manage, thank you."

Alyssa rises, tucking a strand of golden-brown hair behind her ear. "Good afternoon, Mr. Owens," she says quietly.

I had noticed how beautiful her green eyes were before, but in the midday sunlight, they shine like two perfect emeralds.

I give a small nod, careful not to intrude or to reveal my attraction. "We were fortunate to have a few seeds with us when we got here last fall. We are reaping some of the benefits now, but food is most definitely scarce."

"We will help with that as best we can," Alyssa replies simply, her eyes still sparkling in the sunlight. I notice the way she moves, efficient, graceful, and strong, and I can't help but think how marvelous she is, even in this rough, unfamiliar world.

Danielle glances at me and smiles again. "We'll keep at it."

I nod again, tipping my head politely. "Very well. I'll leave you to your work, then."

There is still much work to be done, and Henry Lewis is skilled with a knife. He won't mind helping me clean these rabbits as long as these two beautiful women are the focal point of our conversation while we work.

I step onto the path, the forest floor crunching beneath my boots, and glance back once. Alyssa and Danielle remain absorbed in their tasks, unaware of my departure. I feel a tug of something I cannot name, a mixture of admiration and caution, before setting my mind to the next duty. Survival comes first.

I find Henry near his well, dipping the bucket below. He looks up. "Isaac," he says, a small smile tugging at his lips. "No man here snareth a coney as quickly as ye."

I set the rabbits down beside him. "We'll see how many children we can feed."

Henry shrugs. "Looks like quite a few. Well done, Owens. Have you seen the strangers today, the women?"

"I have," I say. "They're admirable. Hard workers, kind, even under this strain." I hesitate. "I cannot help but notice Alyssa. She carries herself differently than the women I've met. She's not meek, but she's not overwhelmingly outspoken either."

Henry nods. "Aye," he says quietly. "I've been meaning to say, Danielle is the fairest woman I have ever laid eyes on. She hath a fair countenance and a tender heart. It makes the day feel lighter to think of her." He shrugs.

"Aye. I know what you mean."

We begin cleaning the rabbits, scraping and gutting with careful hands. The rhythmic motion steadies me.

When I hear a rustle and a small group of elders passes by, I catch the end of their conversation. "Those women," one of the men says loudly, his voice thick with suspicion. "I heard them. They know too much. Strange remedies, odd ways of doing things…."

Henry straightens. "We rescued them from the ocean," he says firmly. "They mean no harm. They've done nothing but help."

"Best to leave them be," I add, tightening my grip on the rabbit. "They are no threat to us."

The villager snorts, and another mutters under his breath, but they move on. I exchange a glance with Henry and shake my head. Some folks will never see reason.

"Master Owens, Master Lewis, look you here a moment !" a bright, cheerful voice calls as Samuel Tinker bounds toward us, his eyes wide with excitement. "This will make you marvel!"

Henry and I exchange a curious glance and follow him through the garden rows. Alyssa and Danielle are crouched over a small heap of kindling, striking a shard of flint against a bit of steel they must have found. Sparks flare, catching on dry leaves, and within moments, a flame takes hold.

A few settlers draw near, murmuring. It isn't the fire that stirs their wonder—it's that the strangers handle flint and steel as though born to it. Some watch in awe, others cross themselves or whisper uneasy prayers.

"By God," Henry mutters beside me. "They make it look near effortless."

I nod, sensing the tension ripple through the onlookers. A few clap softly, their faces lit by admiration; others step back, muttering of witchcraft. Alyssa and Danielle glance up, calm and steady, as the fire burns bright between them.

Then, as the sparks dance higher—almost leaping from Alyssa's fingertips—the crowd stirs again. Some gasp and cheer; others recoil, whispering behind their hands, torn between reverence and fear.

"Witchcraft!" one woman hisses.

"She's a devil, mark my words," another shouts, her eyes narrowed.

Just then, a tall figure appears at the edge of the throng. Governor William Bradford moves with measured authority, with Captain Miles Standish close behind, his sword at his hip. Bradford's voice carries over the crowd, calm but firm. "Scatter. Quit loitering. Leave the maidens be."

The villagers mutter and grumble but obey, stepping back, with some shaking their heads. A few linger, curious or skeptical, but the immediate threat of confrontation dissolves. I let out a quiet breath. Henry straightens, giving me a small, relieved grin, and I offer a tight-lipped smile back.

Alyssa bends over her fire again, and sparks ignite the tinder without fail. Bradford steps closer, hands behind his back, studying her technique. "Where did you learn to set a fire so fast? Ours rarely catch half so quick." he asks, his voice even but curious.

Alyssa looks up at him calmly, her fingers still deftly moving to coax the flames higher. "In the Indies–near Surat," she replies simply without hesitation.

The governor nods slowly, absorbing the answer without further comment. The fire crackles, warm and steady, casting long shadows over the cleared space.

The governor lets out a quiet chuckle. "The Indies, aye—the land of strange marvels." He nods once, stepping away, and the matter is settled for now.

Henry laughs softly, nudging me with his elbow. "That set a man's blood to moving."

I stand back for a moment, letting the warmth of the fire wash over me, and my eyes settle on Alyssa. She moves with quiet confidence, handling herself as though the wild and the unknown are nothing to fear. Clever, capable, and smart, there's something about her that captivates me in a way I haven't felt in this harsh new world.

I find myself intrigued by her skills and sense, grateful for her presence among us.

EAT YOUR VEGETABLES

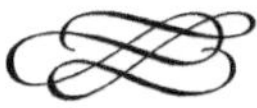

My breath fogs in the morning air as I pull my shawl tighter, trying to ignore the looks we've been getting since yesterday. Every time I catch someone whispering, I hear that word echo in my head—witch.

Danielle falls into step beside me, her cap pulled tight around her dark curls. "Well, Alyssa, congratulations. You've officially been promoted from harmless stranger to village sorceress. Should I start calling you Mistress of Flames?"

I feign a groan. "Don't. I'm already having nightmares about pitch-forks and torches."

She bumps me with her elbow. "Torches they can manage. Pitch-forks, too. But let's be real. If it weren't for us, they'd still be huddled in the dark, staring at damp logs, still trying to get them to catch. You saw their faces when you coaxed that fire up so fast. It was like you'd pulled the sun down into their laps."

"Some of them. Some of them called us witches. We're going to have to think of a better story about where we came from because the questions are going to keep coming the longer we're here," I mutter, lowering my voice as two women pass with only half-full baskets of vegetables. "They don't understand. To them, it's not resourcefulness. It's just unnatural."

Danielle's eyes sparkle with mischief. "Unnatural? Please. What's unnatural is surviving a single New England winter without vitamin C. If they knew half of what we know, they'd faint before they lit the stake."

I can't help laughing. "You're not worried at all?"

"Of course, I'm worried," she says, twirling a loose curl back under her bonnet. "But what are we supposed to do? Play dumb forever? Pretend we don't know how to start a fire so fast, or make pine needle tea, or identify which plants won't kill you? If that makes us witches, then so be it. At least we'll be dry and well-fed witches."

Her confidence warms me more than the sun ever could. Still, I whisper, "I just don't want us to cross a line we can't uncross."

Danielle tilts her head, scanning the meager garden plots. Children cough in the distance, sharp and wet. She sighs. "Lines or no lines, these people are starving, and we know what happens here. We know how many of them will die. We can't sit around and wait. Let's go find something, anything, we can bring back to them."

We slip out past the edge of the clearing, our skirts brushing against dewy grass. The forest swallows the sounds of the colony, replacing them with birdsong and the creak of branches. Danielle hums under her breath, pretending to be carefree, but I notice her eyes darting everywhere.

"Remember the survival unit we did in class?" she asks suddenly. "Sixth graders with their gummy worms and soda, swearing they could live in the wild?"

I laugh. "Yeah, and now here we are, except with less sugar and more scurvy."

She flashes a grin. "Good thing we're a little smarter than twelve-year-olds."

We follow a narrow trail until the trees thin. We come around a corner, and I gasp. Ahead, a small group of Wampanoag women bend over neat rows of early autumn crops. Their baskets are already filled with corn, squash, and beans. Sunlight washes over them as they move with practiced grace.

"Okay," Danielle whispers. "Rule number one, let's try not to scare them."

I nod, my heart thudding. We step forward slowly, our palms open, smiling gently. The women glance up, cautious but not hostile. One raises a hand in greeting.

Danielle whispers, quick as ever, "We have nothing to barter, so let's just look pitiful. We're good at pitiful."

"Don't make me laugh right now," I whisper back.

I elbow her, fighting a nervous laugh, and bow my head slightly toward the women. I point at the baskets, then at my mouth, miming hunger. The Wampanoag women exchange amused looks, their eyes softer now, and one offers us a squash with a small, knowing smile.

Warmth rises in my chest. Even across centuries and languages, kindness speaks loudest.

Another woman offers a whole basket of corn, holding it out to us with a quiet word I don't understand. Her expression is kind, her deep brown eyes shimmer, and my shoulders loosen just a little. I reach out slowly, my hands open, but before I can take it, a sharp voice cuts through the trees.

"Don't talk to them!"

I jerk around. Isaac strides out from the woods with Henry close behind. Both of them look ready for a fight, their muskets slung across their shoulders, their faces tight with alarm.

Isaac's eyes flash at me. "Step back, Mistress Montgomery and Mistress Whitman. Now."

"They're not dangerous," I protest, clutching the squash against my chest like a shield. "Look at them. They're women, just like us."

Henry's hand hovers near his musket. "You don't know that. You've no notion what they intend."

Danielle threads her arms through the handle of the basket of corn. "Oh, please. If they intended to harm us, don't you think we'd be tied up already? Or worse?"

Isaac stiffens. "This is no jest, Mistress Whitman."

She smirks. "I wasn't jesting. I'm just pointing out the obvious. These women have baskets of food, not weapons."

The Wampanoag women watch the exchange, murmuring to one another with tension in their tone. They don't back away, though. They hold their ground with a strength and dignity that makes my throat tighten. One of them takes a step closer, extending her hand as a gesture of peace and friendship.

I take her hand and squeeze it once, nodding that I understand. Turning back to Isaac, I say, "See? They're trying to share."

His brow furrows, not in anger but in thought. "They do look peaceable," he admits.

Danielle shoots him a bright grin. "Exactly! Now, if we could stop talking about them as though they're not right here, that would be great."

He blushes, muttering, "I suppose you're right. My apologies."

The Wampanoag women begin filling the basket they've given us with more corn, beans, and a few more squash. They gesture for us to take it, and I bow my head gratefully. "Thank you," I whisper, not caring that they can't understand the words. Gratitude, I've learned, speaks its own language.

When the women finally step back, waving their hands in farewell, Danielle and I bow our heads slightly and press our hands to our chests, letting our gestures speak the words our voices can't.

Now, our basket is brimming, Danielle beams at Isaac and Henry. "See? No witchcraft, no arrows, no bloodshed, just neighbors helping neighbors."

Henry chuckles under his breath, though Isaac shakes his head. "Neighbors or no, you'd do well to be cautious. This land holds more dangers than you can imagine."

"Perhaps so," Danielle replies, hefting the basket onto her hip. "But it also holds friends, and right now, I think we could use as many of those as we can get."

A fragile hope stirs in my chest. We're not as alone here as we thought.

By the time the village comes into view, Henry has gently lifted the heavy basket from Danielle's arms, carrying it with a careful, chivalrous strength. Isaac steps up beside me, offering to take the squash I've been holding. He puts it in his satchel and slings it back over his shoulder. Danielle and I walk between them, exchanging relieved glances, already bracing for the questions that await.

The center of Plymouth stirs with its usual afternoon bustle. Women stir pots, children chase each other, and men repair fences or haul wood. As soon as Henry sets the basket down near the common fire, heads turn toward us.

"What's this?" calls a tall man, pausing mid-swing from splitting logs. His voice carries suspicion, and Isaac leans close to murmur, "That's Edward Fuller. There's ever a complaint about his tongue."

Before I can answer, Edward's wife steps forward, wiping her hands on her apron. "Didst though steal that from the heathens?"

Danielle lifts her chin. "They are most definitely not heathens, and they gave it to us, kindly and freely."

A ripple goes through the crowd. A wiry woman with sharp eyes crosses her arms. Isaac whispers again, low, "That's Priscilla Mullins. Best keep on her good side. For, she's quick to call out sin."

Priscilla narrows her gaze at Danielle and me. "First fire far more quickly than expected. Now food from the savages. What manner of women art though?"

My pulse skips. Around us, children gather close to their mothers, and a few men shift uneasily, as if standing near us might invite trouble.

"We are women who wish to help," I say, keeping my voice calm. "These vegetables will fill empty bellies. Is that not the Lord's provision?"

"Aye, or Satan's snare," mutters a gray-bearded man from the back.

Isaac doesn't bother whispering this time, he just says aloud, "That's Goodman Clarke. He thinks every shadow hides a devil."

Danielle folds her arms. "Ah. The devil always wants to send me squash. I say Mr. Devil, please send me a mountain of gingerbread, but he wants me to eat my vegetables."

A few children giggle before their mothers shush them, and I have a difficult time stifling my laughter.

Goodman Clark scowls deeper. "Thou darest mock me? Witches are known for trickery, for seeming helpful until they have you by the throat."

"That's enough," Henry says sharply, stepping forward. His usually mild-mannered expression is tight with anger. "I was there. The Indians gave these freely. These women are guilty of no offense"

Bradford himself has appeared now, drawn by the noise. Miles Standish is at his side, his eyes scanning the circle of villagers.

"What is the cause of this uproar?" Bradford asks, his voice firm.

One of the men points a finger at Danielle and me. "Governor, these women meddle where they ought not, teaching strange ways, taking counsel with savages, giving orders like men. 'Tis not fitting."

Bradford's gaze fixes on me, heavy as stone. I swallow hard, feeling Danielle stiffen at my side. Around us, the whispers rise louder—witch, pagan, devil, dangerous.

Bradford lifts his hand, and the crowd quiets enough for his voice to carry. "You say the natives gave this freely. I would hear it plain from your own mouths. Owens, Lewis, what did you see?"

Henry clears his throat, squaring his shoulders. "Governor, I saw no harm done. They met us in the woods by coincidence, the Indian women carrying their harvest, a much bountiful one indeed. They offered food in peace."

Isaac nods stiffly. "Aye. They gave squash, beans, and corn, and even shook hands to show their goodwill. I cannot say it was ill-meant."

Standish narrows his eyes, one hand still resting on his sword. "Or perhaps it was meant to beguile you. Savages have a hundred faces."

"They are not savages," I say before I can stop myself. My voice rings too loud, and all heads turn. "They are the Wampanoag people. Their tribe members tend their land with great skill. They hunt and forge, they fish, and they know the earth's ways better than anyone here. If we could accept and embrace our differences, these people could be friends and teachers."

A hush falls. Bradford regards me closely, thoughtfully. Standish studies me as if weighing whether my words are foolish or bold.

At last, Bradford says, "There is sense in what Mistress Montgomery speaks. If they mean to trade, if they come in peace, we would be wise to listen. We have not yet learned how to thrive on this soil."

Standish exhales through his nose but gives a short nod. "I will not trust them, not yet. Alas, if they can aid us through the winter, it's no small matter."

Murmurs ripple through the crowd. Some nod, while others shake their heads furiously. Goodman Clarke spits into the dirt. "Mark my words. They'll turn on us before spring."

Priscilla Mullins lifts her chin. "And these women speak too boldly. It's not a woman's place to tell men how to deal with heathens!"

Danielle flashes a grin that makes my stomach twist with worry. "Perhaps it is no one's place to starve when help is at hand." She crouches by the basket, pulling out beans and a squash, holding them out to a pair of children who stare with hunger in their eyes. "And who are you, oh toothless one, calling anyone a heathen?"

Priscilla's face turns bright red, and she stomps off in a furious storm of embarrassment and rage.

"I think you just earned us a true enemy," I whisper to Danielle.

"I hope so," she replies with a sigh. "I'd hate to be called a witch by a friend."

"Witch," I whisper.

Danielle grins and raises her voice so the crowd can hear her. "Children first, please. Come and get some of this healthy food. But please, wash your hands and the food first in clean water. By clean, I mean water that has been boiled and cooled. It will keep sickness away."

The children glance at their mothers. Some of the women hesitate, pulling their children back.

"Do not heed her," one of them hisses. "She makes herself mistress over us all!"

More voices rise, sharp with indignation.

"Who are they to give commands?"

"Washing hands, like some papist ritual!"

"Women ought to be silent!"

Bradford raises his voice again, but the tide of muttering swells around us. Danielle presses the squash into the hands of a child before her mother snatches it away. I can feel the heat of angry stares pressing in, as though the crowd itself means to swallow us whole.

I glance at Henry and Isaac, both caught between us and their neighbors. My heart thunders. What began as a simple gift of food is now a storm, and the two of us stand at its center.

Bradford's hand stills the murmuring once again. His eyes fix sharply on me and then on Danielle. "What do you mean by telling us how to live? Are these rituals you have picked up in India? Is that how you spoke with these tribal savages? You name them Wampanoag. How is it you know their tribe when most here have scarce seen a native face?"

Standish adds, his tone clipped, "And more, how came you to understand their meaning? Did they speak in English to you?"

The crowd leans closer, hungry for answers.

Danielle and I lock eyes. For a heartbeat, neither of us breathes. Then, Danielle steps forward, smooth as ever. "Governor Bradford, with all due respect, we have traveled more broadly than most here could dream. Alyssa's father served in the military overseas, and in his travels, he took us with him. We met many people who spoke many tongues. It is no strange occurrence for us to see their manner, their ways, and quickly familiarize ourselves within their culture."

I nod quickly, adding, "And often, when people share kindness, they need little speech. A hand to the heart, a smile, the offering of food—it is plain enough. We saw goodwill in their faces, and that is how we were able to know one another's meaning."

Bradford's gaze narrows, weighing on us. A hush falls, broken only by the crackle of the fire and the restless shifting of feet.

A woman's sharp voice cuts through. "Hear them boast!"

An elderly man shakes his head. "Travelers, they call themselves. I say deceivers. They speak too freely. Mark me, Governor. It is witchcraft."

The word hisses through the crowd like a spark leaping to dry kindling. Witchcraft.

Danielle throws up her hands. "Oh, for pity's sake! If washing your hands and eating beans makes us witches, then we are the worst sort, clean and well-fed!"

Laughter bubbles from a few children, quickly hushed by their mothers.

Standish's hand tightens on his sword hilt, though his expression is more irritated than fearful. "Enough of this chatter. We can't starve, nor can we quarrel till winter devours us. If these women bring food, we take it. If they bring folly, the Lord will judge."

Bradford nods slowly. "Aye. Let it be so. We will test what they offer and see if it brings health or harm."

Yet, the crowd still murmurs uneasily. Questioning eyes follow Danielle and me. Even with Bradford's word, suspicion coils tighter around us like a noose.

Danielle leans closer, her voice low, for my ears only. "Well," she mutters. "I suppose we've bought ourselves a little time, but this fire we've lit is not going out soon."

As the crowd slowly scatters, our baskets lighter and tempers still simmering, I clutch the hem of my shawl and draw a long breath. We've done more today than gather food. We've crossed a threshold. We've met the Wampanoag, looked into their eyes, and felt no fear, only kindness.

I'm beginning to truly believe that's why Danielle and I were flung here—four hundred years from home—to stand in the middle, to be the hands that bridge the space between two worlds. The thought relieves me only slightly, threading with the ache of missing my parents, James, and Chloe.

I don't know if I'll ever see them again, but as I glance at Danielle's quick smile and the wary hope in the faces around us, I feel that if we can't yet go home, then maybe our task is to help this fragile place survive.

IT IS WELL

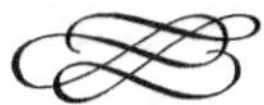

Isaac

THE HEAT HITS ME BEFORE I EVEN OPEN MY EYES. SMOKE CURLS INTO the small chamber where I've been sleeping, acrid and sharp in my nostrils. I sit up, looking out the window. Flames lick the thatched roof of the neighboring house, the Hawkins place, spitting sparks into the wind that carries them toward the rest of the village.

"Fire!" someone shouts.

My heart jolts as I scramble off my straw mattress, coughing as the smoke thickens. The smell of burning wood fills the night, and panic thrums like a drum in my chest.

I'm barely out the door when I see the Tinker family already at work, buckets in hand. Thomas is tossing water from the well, shouting instructions.

"Isaac! Grab a bucket!" Henry calls, sprinting past me with Danielle at his side and Alyssa following close behind.

I seize a pail from the line forming at the well, water sloshing over the rim as I run to the front of the burning house. Flames crackle through the roof, sparks scattering across the dry ground. I dump the water, my heart hammering, then race back for another.

"Keep the line moving!" Bradford's voice cuts through the din. He stands a few yards away with rolled sleeves, his face pale but resolute. Standish prowls near the edge of the crowd, axe in hand, ready to tear away anything that might catch fire next.

Danielle is in the yard, stamping out embers with the edge of a shovel, while Alyssa tosses wet blankets over the flames, dragging them back before the fire can leap further. Henry grunts under the weight of a full bucket, sloshing water over the wall of fire.

The villagers form a chain, passing buckets and dousing sparks that drift too close to the neighboring homes. The night is alive with the roar of flames, the hiss of water, the clatter of wood, and the shouted commands of Bradford and Standish.

A cry cuts through the noise. Mrs. Hawkins screams as her small home, near the edge of the settlement, collapses into a burning heap. Everyone halts for a heart-stopping second, but no one is hurt. Relief washes over me, though I feel a sting at her loss. There's nothing we can do but mourn the home while the fire threatens to spread.

Alyssa and Danielle move toward Mrs. Hawkins, pulling her away from the wreckage, offering comfort as best they can. Henry wraps a dry blanket around her shoulders. Thomas Tinker points to a cleared space nearby. "We'll help them rebuild. Not tonight, but at dawn."

I pause for a moment, my chest heaving, watching the flames finally die down. Sparks still drift skyward like fireflies gone mad, but the worst is over. Bradford and Standish confer in low voices, scanning the village for the source of the fire.

As the last sparks die, the villagers slowly scatter, clearing debris and checking on neighbors. The Hawkins family is guided to the parson's spare room for the night. Thomas and Ann Tinker offer what blankets, prayers, and comfort they can. I pause near the well, catching my breath, and finally speak.

"Mistress Montgomery, Mistress Whitman, and Henry, would you like to join me for a warm cup?" I ask, nodding toward my small cottage. "Tea might steady our nerves."

Alyssa flashes a quick grin. "Sounds civilized enough. I'll take it."

Inside my house, I start with the kettle while Danielle and Alyssa find seats, brushing soot from their skirts. Henry looks through my stockpile of herbs for something suitable enough to calm us.

He grabs a small bundle of chamomile and a few sprigs of mint from the shelf, tossing them into a kettle. The fragrant steam rises immediately, filling the room with a gentle, soothing scent. I let them steep, the delicate aroma promising a calm respite after the chaos outside.

"I'm glad no one was hurt," Alyssa says softly, taking the cup I hand her. "That could have been much worse."

"True," Danielle agrees. "It's frightening how quickly everything changes here."

I fill a cup for Danielle, Henry, then myself, and sit opposite the women. Henry glances at the maidens. "Forgive my boldness, but I must needs ask—what is it you two intend? You've set the villagers ill at ease, and such stirrings may bring danger."

Danielle arches a brow. "Upsetting them? Whatever do you mean?" She's smiling, and yet, I cannot tell if she jests.

"Well," Henry begins, rubbing the back of his neck, "you're telling them to wash their hands before they eat and to boil the water to wash the vegetables before they cook them. You showed them a faster way to make fire, and you've been encouraging friendship with the Indians." He looks between us, concern enveloping his features. "'Tis all well-meant, I know, but the people murmur. They take your goodness amiss, and such talk breeds trouble. It may turn them from you."

Alyssa leans forward. "Isn't it all worth it if it saves lives? If it helps children grow stronger and keeps families from starving?"

Danielle nods, smiling. "We know the risk, but what we can teach them could mean the difference between sickness and health, hunger and hope. I'd rather be disliked for doing good than admired for doing nothing."

Henry exhales slowly, shaking his head, though a small smile tugs at his lips. "I cannot say I have your courage. It is a most worthy deed.

You show the charity of true hearts. For myself, I should lack the courage to abide such peril of men's anger."

"You've taken risks for us already," I say quietly. "You have laid your repute and your very safety in peril for strangers. Such sacrifice is no small virtue."

"We don't do it for praise," Alyssa says, her striking green eyes fixed on me. "It would mean a great deal if you agreed with us and showed your support while we're trying to help the villagers. If we can help even a few, teach them something that keeps them alive through the winter, then it's worth the whispers and the suspicion. And, perhaps, we'll build trust with them in the end. That's all we can hope for."

"If anyone deserves that trust, it's you two. Bold and unafraid, even when the village might rise against you," I reply.

"Fear doesn't guide us," Danielle says. "Responsibility does, and if we have the knowledge to make a difference, then we'd be worse than cowardly not to act."

Henry exhales, running a hand down his face, then shakes his head slowly, a faint smile tugging at his lips. "I see. You're both brave and stubborn. I suppose that's what this village needs."

I stand, setting down my empty cup. Tonight brings a fragile calm, the sort that follows exhaustion and relief. "Come," I say, gesturing toward the Tinker house nearby. "We'll walk you back. You've earned a moment's rest."

Henry and I escort Alyssa and Danielle back to the Tinker house. Because of the ash lying about, I offer my arm to Alyssa, and she slips hers through, her warmth sending a lightning bolt straight through me. Some might call it improper to stand so close to her, but it is late, and no one else is about. She leans slightly closer, and I feel the pull, an unspoken spark between us. By the time we reach the Tinker door, I don't want to let go. I press a little closer, and her quick inhale tells me she feels it, too. Once the women are safely inside, I bid Henry farewell and turn toward my own home, but I can't shake the memory of Alyssa, the warmth of her arm, the keen intelligence in her words, the way her presence makes my pulse race. I lie in bed, staring at the ceiling, my heart hammering, thinking about how impossibly alive she makes me feel.

Alyssa Montgomery, brave, brilliant, and she draws me as the lodestone draws the iron. She has me caught in her circle, as the moon is bound to the earth, and I have no desire to escape.

❧

DAWN BARELY BRUSHES THE SKY WHEN I STEP OUTSIDE. THE CRISP AIR bites at my cheeks, and smoke from last night still lingers, clinging stubbornly to the ground. Today, everyone will pitch in to help the Hawkins family build a new home. Some men stack wood near the center of the village. Tools clatter as others sharpen axes, and the smell of sawdust and wet earth fills the air.

As I carry a beam toward the framework already rising, voices drift across the settlement. I freeze mid-step.

"It's those women! Mistress Montgomery and Mistress Whitman —they were messing about near the Hawkins' house and look what has transpired!" a man hisses to someone else, sharp with accusation.

"They've been teaching fire tricks and charms," another mutters. "Nothing good comes of it. Witches, mark my words."

My stomach twists. I want to run toward the voices, to set the record straight, but I hold back. The villagers are still too riled, too quick to lay blame for what they don't understand. I tighten my grip on the beam, feeling the weight of responsibility pressing down on me.

A flash of worry cuts through me. They acted to save lives last night. Yet, already, the seeds of mistrust are being sown.

I glance across the yard and spot Henry guiding Samuel Tinker, showing him how to nail a plank into place safely. His eyes meet mine, and in that small look, I sense he's heard some of the whispers, too. When I approach, he shakes his head slightly, muttering under his breath, "Le them speak their fill—they understand not what they've witnessed.

I nod, grateful for his sensibility, as Alyssa and Danielle approach the Hawkins' lot. My chest tightens at the thought of them facing suspicion and scorn even here, yet they still refuse to back down.

Hours pass in steady, exhausting labor. Planks are hoisted, nails driven, walls squared and braced under the relentless sun. The initial burst of energy fades into measured, careful movements. Voices grow sparse, and even the usual teasing and laughter are swallowed by the strain. Fatigue settles over everyone.

When the sun hangs low over the nearly built Hawkins house, the villagers move with slow, weary motions—beams lifted, hammers striking, sweat dripping into the dust of the day. Everyone is quiet, the rhythm of work dulling even the chatter that usually fills the air when Danielle sets down the log she's carrying, and tilts her head.

A clear note rises into a melody from her lips, carrying a story no one in the village has ever heard before. It is the song of a man lost at sea, battered by storm and wave, his life at the mercy of the deep. Yet, despite the fear, the despair, there is peace, for he trusts in Jesus, and his heart is calm.

Alyssa joins in, her pure voice weaving seamlessly with Danielle's, lifting into a perfect harmony that threads through the weariness of the workers.

The song grows, strangely beautiful enough to make the villagers stop and listen, and it's comforting enough to draw some nearer.

When Danielle begins the reprieve, "It is well—"

Alyssa answers, "It is well—"

Danielle continues, "With my soul—"

Alyssa's voice soars, "With my soul—"

The two repeat, layering their voices like sunlight on still water, each note carrying serenity and calm, each echo a balm for weariness.

A hush spreads over the crowd. Hammers pause mid-swing, shoulders sag, and eyes lift from splintered beams. Even the skeptical villagers, the ones who have whispered doubts, the ones who have questioned the women aloud and accusingly, stop to listen. Some stare, some whisper prayers under their breath, and some wipe tears from their cheeks.

The song continues, gentle and unwavering, flowing over the tired men and women like a river through the settlement.

Danielle sings, "Whatever my lot, the Lord has taught me to say—"

And Alyssa answers, "It is well. It is well with my soul."

The melody lingers in the air, and I watch the subtle shifts in the villagers' faces. The fear, the suspicion, the sharp words are softening, replaced by awe and quiet gratitude. Slowly, carefully, hope threads itself through the tired hearts. They see that these women are not meddlesome or dangerous, and that they are gifts, bringing comfort where chaos has reigned.

I set down my hammer and stand still, listening until the last echo fades into the evening. Alyssa and Danielle lower their heads, their faces calm but radiant, the unspoken pride in their eyes speaking volumes. The house is still unfinished, the work far from complete, but the village feels lighter. For a moment, all the turmoil, all the fear of yesterday, is held at bay by the simple, haunting refrain.

I wipe my hands, my chest still thrumming, and realize that even in the quiet, even in exhaustion, the world feels just a little more whole.

LEAVING THE FUTURE BEHIND

Alyssa

We trail a few steps behind the Tinkers, my arms aching from lifting beams all day. Dirt and sweat cling to my skin, but I feel lighter somehow. The Hawkins house is standing, mostly, and for once, the village seems less tense. Long shadows stretch across our path as Danielle walks beside me, quiet for a moment, letting the evening settle over us.

"You know," I say, keeping my voice low. "I am always amazed by your ability to think on your feet. That song… I don't even know how you thought of it." I shake my head in wonder, the memory of our voices rising over the laborers so vivid in my mind. "A hymn, Danielle. Singing 'It Is Well with My Soul' like that—I think it worked. Every single one of them was touched, even the ones who had been whispering about witchcraft."

Danielle glances at me, grinning, the corners of her eyes crinkling in amusement. "Honestly, I thought they'd join in once they learned the lyrics. It seemed like a peaceful choice, at least. You know, I thought we could give them something to focus on besides fear and suspicion."

I laugh, brushing a strand of hair from my face. "That was genius, absolute genius. I can't believe we remembered most of the words."

"Oh, come on," she chides me. "We sang that song a million times, ever since Sunday school when we were kids. I just think it will be exhausting trying to prove ourselves every day. Despite every small gesture of goodwill we've made, every lesson we've tried to teach them, still, suspicion lingers. But today, with the song, it felt like something shifted. I could see it in their eyes, even the difficult ones. They were listening, feeling something, maybe hope."

I glance at her, gratitude and admiration welling up in my chest. "You're brilliant, Danielle. Truly. I don't know what I'd do without you. You always think so clearly, even when everything else is crazy."

She chuckles, shaking her head. "You flatter me. And you—if anyone notices the work we do or the words we sing, it's because you believe in it, too. You lend my creativity the brains and brawn we need to achieve our goals."

We fall into silence, walking in rhythm with the Tinkers up ahead. My chest still hums with the memory of the song, the harmony between us, the way the village paused to listen.

"Maidens?" Mrs. Tinker's voice drifts from the path ahead. "That was a beautiful song. I've never heard it before, and yet it certainly spoke to me. Perhaps, if you wish, you could teach it in church next Sunday?"

Danielle and I exchange a look, our eyes widening, mirroring each other's sudden realization. The song we chose is centuries ahead of this time, and yet, somehow, we've shared it here, with them.

"Of course, Goody Tinker," I reply, a small, incredulous smile tugging at my lips.

Danielle laughs and whispers, "Well, I suppose that makes today even more remarkable. Not just building a house, but leaving a little bit more of the future behind."

We follow the Tinkers into their modest home after the day's labors. Thomas and Jane fuss over the meal, ladling meager soup into wooden bowls, the aroma rich and comforting. We eat slowly, the clatter of spoons and the murmur of conversation a gentle rhythm after the hectic day. Danielle leans back, wiping a streak of dirt from her forehead, and I can't help but be amazed by the way she thought on her feet today, even though we've been working so hard and are so incredibly tired.

After dinner, we help clear the table and then say goodnight to the Tinkers. In the small loft, Danielle and I prepare for bed, washing the grit of sawdust and sweat from our skin. I crawl under the blankets, the fabric scratchy but warm, and Danielle follows shortly after. I close my eyes, trying to hold onto the calm the song brought to the village, but the feeling eludes me.

The melody we sang, the harmony we shared, soothed them, yes, but it can't end the ache in my chest. My thoughts drift home, to my family, to the life that feels impossibly distant. For all the good we did today, for all the hope we stirred, it is not well with my soul. Not yet, and as the night deepens, I press my eyes closed, silently wishing Danielle and I were home.

THE NEXT MORNING, WE MOVE THROUGH THE BRAMBLES, GATHERING small clusters of ripe autumn raspberries, our fingers sticky with juice. Danielle sings "Somewhere Over the Rainbow," and I let her voice ease my thoughts as we bend over low bushes, filling our baskets.

Suddenly, a shout carries across the clearing. Young Samuel Tinker comes running toward us, his face pale and tight with worry. "Mistress Montgomery! Mistress Whitman!" His voice trembles. "You must come quickly. The Connors... they've been found dead this morning, and the children are weak and sick."

My stomach turns. Danielle and I exchange a look, unspoken understanding passing between us, and we race back to the village without a second thought.

By the time we reach the village, a small crowd has gathered near the Connors' modest home. A man in a dark coat, his satchel slung across his shoulder, moves with careful authority.

"There are four children here," he says. "They're alive but emaciated, weak, and suffering from severe dehydration and malnutrition. They will not survive long without care."

"That's the surgeon, Master Fuller," Samuel explains.

I step closer instinctively. Danielle stands beside me, her jaw set, her eyes sharp with resolve. "We can help," I say. "We'll stay with them, nurse them back to health. Whatever they need, we'll do it."

Dr. Fuller's eyes move between us, searching for hesitation, but he finds none. "They are on the edge of life, and their condition is delicate. You will need to move quickly, feed them as much as you can, and help them drink."

Danielle nods. "We understand. We'll do everything we can."

"Aye. Very well, I'll leave them in your care," he says.

I can't help but wonder why no one seems to object to our taking charge of these children. Maybe it's not trust or confidence in us at all but simply that the villagers are too worn down by their own families and daily struggles to take on four more mouths. They're exhausted and stretched too thin, and in their eyes, maybe we're just willing to step in where they can't. Or maybe they've already decided these children won't survive, and it doesn't matter much who tries. I gulp, the thought sickening me.

"I knew you'd help them," Samuel says, his eyes full of gratitude.

"You were right to come looking for us, Sam," I reply. "Anytime someone needs help, you come and find Danielle and me," I add, my tone firm.

I feel the weight of responsibility settle on my shoulders, but alongside it, a fierce determination. These kids, so small and helpless, will have us beside them now. We won't abandon them.

We step inside the house. The children lie on their pallets or sit on chairs, their faces pale, their bodies fragile from weeks without proper food. I move carefully among them, offering spoonfuls of the fresh berries and sips of water. Each small bite brings a faint color back to their cheeks, and the tiniest signs of hope flare in their eyes.

Danielle moves from one to another, adjusting blankets, smoothing hair, and whispering gentle, comforting words. The room is hushed except for the rustle of fabric and the sips of water.

I glance at her, a thought striking me. "Danielle, let's step outside for a bit. We could look for mushrooms or anything else nutritious we can forage. A few minutes in the sun might do us some good, and maybe we can gather something more to help the children."

"You're right. Mushrooms, nuts—there has to be something we can feed them."

The forest offers small treasures: walnuts, wild greens, and hidden among the roots, mushrooms. We move carefully, recognizing the colors and shapes that we know are safe. Each mushroom we pick feels like a small victory, a chance to nourish the Connors. The damp earth smells rich and alive, and I can't help but marvel at Danielle's quick eyes and steady hands as she identifies the safest and plumpest fungi.

"This is the perfect time of year for chanterelles and honey mushrooms. I hadn't even thought about it, but the pilgrims wouldn't know that these are good for them."

"You're right. I'm glad my grandfather taught us when we were kids which ones are safe to eat and which ones are poisonous."

"Some of my favorite memories are of visiting your grandma and grandpa at their farm." Her voice trails off. I catch the shadow in her eyes, knowing she's mourning the chance she never had to know her own grandparents.

Danielle never had any of that—no grandparents to run to, no steady family to lean on. Her parents were too far gone in their own struggles, and she grew up an only child, carrying more loneliness than any kid should. I think that's where her deep well of compassion comes from, why she's such a good teacher, and why she's out here in the woods with me now, searching for mushrooms to feed starving children. She knows what hunger feels like. When she wasn't at my house, there were nights she went without dinner.

"Alyssa, I don't know why I'm even saying this." Danielle's voice interrupts my thoughts. "But… I think I'm falling for Henry. I can't stop daydreaming about the little things like walking beside him, hearing him laugh, even just holding a plank of wood together while we work. It's ridiculous with everything going on, but I feel it anyway."

I smile at her. "It's not ridiculous at all. I've noticed. You have that dreamy look when he's near."

"It feels wrong, in a way, to think about such things now, but I can't help imagining a life with him. The little ordinary moments, even in the middle of this craziness...."

I shake my head, admiring her honesty. "You're brave, Danielle, in more ways than one, and maybe it's not wrong at all. Sparks like that keep us alive, even when the world feels dark. Maybe he's the reason we're here."

She glances at me, a faint blush on her cheeks. "What about you, Alyssa? You and Isaac...."

I shrug, though my chest tightens. "He's incredibly handsome, patient, and he's the kind of man a person can trust without question. Being near him, working side by side, feels almost safe, even though we're four hundred years in the past. Somehow."

We share a smile, and for a moment, the burdens of the day lift, replaced by something softer, something like romantic whimsy.

Our baskets heavy with mushrooms, berries, and wild greens, Danielle and I make our way back to the Connor house. I can already imagine the children's gaunt faces lighting up at the sight of wholesome, nourishing, and warm food for the first time in days.

Henry and Isaac appear ahead of us, walking slowly along the path. Henry's eyes find Danielle immediately, and a faint, nervous smile plays at his lips. "Mistress Williams, I must fetch wood before nightfall. You're welcome to walk with me, if you've a mind for air."

Danielle looks at me first. "Have you got this?" she whispers, handing me her basket.

"Of course. Go ahead. I'll stay here and fry up these mushrooms for the children." My words carry warmth and encouragement, and I see the excitement beaming across Danielle's face. She nods, her cheeks pink, and falls into step alongside Henry.

Isaac turns to me. "Would you like some help with that?" His voice carries its usual reassurance as he reaches for the baskets.

"Thank you," I reply, grateful for the offer. Together, we enter the Connor house. The kitchen is small and modest, but the hearth is ready, and the warmth of the fire promises more than just heat. It promises a meal, a sense of normalcy, and a comfort the kids have not known for days.

Isaac leans over the basket, peering at the fungi. "What are these?" he asks, curiosity in his voice.

"Chanterelles and honey mushrooms," I reply, picking one up carefully. "They're safe to eat, and full of nutrients these children need."

He nods, impressed. "You're extraordinary. I wouldn't have known these were safe to ingest."

We set the baskets on the table, the mushrooms earthy and firm, the greens bright and fresh, the walnuts like tiny gems in the fading light. I pull a skillet from a hook next to the hearth and clean the mushrooms in some of the fresh water we brought in earlier. Then, I slice them up while Isaac washes the greens and rinses them before he sets to work cracking up the walnuts.

As the skillet heats, the mushrooms sizzle and release their rich aroma, filling the room with the smell of sustenance. Isaac stirs the greens gently, sprinkling a pinch of salt, and I crush a few of this morning's berries into a bowl to put atop a loaf of bread one of the villagers brought earlier. Their juice fills the loaf with natural sweetness. Together, we create a meal that is simple but rich with care and attention.

I spoon the mushrooms and greens onto plates, adding berries on the side for sweetness, and add a piece of bread to each. The children watch with wide eyes, their hunger obvious in the way they lean forward and devour the food.

Isaac moves beside me, arranging the plates with equal care. As I lean to hand one of the little girls a plate, a loose strand of hair falls across my cheek. Isaac brushes it back gently, tucking it behind my ear. The motion is so slight, so fleeting, that it could have gone unnoticed, but it makes my pulse quicken, and for a heartbeat, the warmth of the kitchen fades to a private moment between us.

I look up at him, catching the faintest hint of a smile, but he doesn't linger, doesn't speak. Yet, even as I continue serving plates and refilling cups, the memory of that simple gesture clings to me, a reminder that amid the sorrow and toil, there is a thread of something romantic weaving its way into the long days.

The room is filled with the rhythm of forks against plates, when a sharp knock at the door startles me. Isaac glances at me, and hurries to open it.

Priscilla Mullins stands there, her arms crossed, her lips tight, scanning the room as if she's judging everything. A few other villagers, mostly women, hover behind her, curiosity and suspicion written on their faces.

"Well," Priscilla begins, her voice thin with disapproval. "I see you've taken charge of these children." She steps inside, her eyes moving to the beds and chairs, then to the children eating their dinner. "I hope you're tending to them properly."

I offer a small, measured smile. "We're giving them whatever nourishment we can find. They've been without proper food for days."

Her gaze narrows. "I should think berries and greens are fine enough, but what's this?" She points to the small plate of leftover mushrooms, still warm from the skillet. Her brow furrows, the scowl on her face highlighting the fact that she is, in fact, missing quite a few teeth.

"Mushrooms. They're safe," I say quickly. "We found them in the woods. They're nutritious and will help the children regain strength."

Priscilla steps closer, leaning slightly over the table. "I've not seen the like of them. Are you sure they'll do no harm to the children? They might well be deadly." She lets the words hang in the air, sharp with suspicion, and straightens again, her arms folded.

I swallow, keeping my tone steady. "I've checked carefully. They're edible. They'll give them the nourishment they need."

The villagers exchange uneasy glances, murmuring among themselves. Priscilla fixes me with a long, judging stare, her lips a tight line. "We shall see."

And with that, she steps back, still eyeing everything with disapproval, as if she's daring me to fail.

I wonder, not for the first time, if saving these people really is my destiny, or whether I should try to go back to 2025 because obviously some of them don't want our help. Yet, as I look at Isaac, at the children, and even at the stubborn defiance in nasty Priscilla Mullins, I feel a tug on my heartstrings for all of them.

WOMEN TO TEACH

Isaac

Henry and I sit near the hissing morning fire in the hearth, but the pot gives off little scent, only thin porridge, stretched too far with water.

I've offered Henry breakfast at my house, as his supplies are running even lower than mine. He graciously accepted, despite the meager meal. We eat slowly, the silence between us carrying the weight of last night.

Priscilla's voice still rings in my ears, sharp and sure as she accused Alyssa of poisoning the children with her mushrooms and of bringing wickedness among us. I see Alyssa's pretty face in my mind, and the way she held her chin high, though I could read the hurt in her eyes.

Henry shakes his head. "I can't abide how some of the villagers are speaking such lies against our new friends."

"Nor can I," I answer at once. My voice sounds too fierce in the quiet room, but I don't soften it. "Neither of those women is dangerous. They're certainly peculiar, but in an endearing way. Alas, neither of them has an evil bone in their body."

Henry leans back, pushing the empty bowl aside. "While I walked with Danielle last evening, she told me about the children she taught where she lived before. She has a keen mind, Isaac. I have never met a woman who speaks so plainly, nor with such knowledge."

I lift a brow. "You have grown fond of her already."

"Perhaps," he admits, though his smile lingers. "She is unlike any woman I have ever known. And Mistress Whitman, too. Both of them carry themselves as though they come from another world, one where women aren't forced into meekness."

I stir the porridge in my bowl, though I have no appetite. "Do you think they will stay among us or strike out to find the rest of their kin? Surely, they would like to rejoin their party if there are any survivors."

Henry folds his arms across his chest, thinking. "If it were me, I would seek my family. Yet, the season will turn soon. The woods are no gentle place for women alone, especially in winter."

I glance at the small fire fighting to keep the chill from the room. Beyond these walls, children lie weak in their beds, their mothers wringing cloths and whispering prayers, and still, our stores grow lighter.

"Aye. Yet, they may not survive here either. There is not enough food," I say, "And too few men left strong enough to fish the bay or bring in game from the forest. The women and children can't bear that burden."

Henry's jaw tightens. "We won't last the winter on nuts and berries. We need meat."

I meet his eyes across the table. "Aye. Shall we hunt today, you and I, and any others with strength left? If we wait, hunger will finish us."

He leans forward, resting his forearms on the table, a glint of resolve in his eyes. "We should. Shall we go and tell the women where we will be?"

I nod. "They should know where we're heading before we leave."

Henry and I leave my cabin and walk the short path to the Connor home. I knock on the door. Alyssa answers it, looking as radiant as ever, though her apron is wet and a wisp of golden hair peaks out from under her cap.

"Good morning. What a pleasant surprise," she says, welcoming us into the room.

Inside, the rhythmic clatter of dishes reaches us as Danielle washes up after breakfast.

"Good morning," Danielle says, glancing up from her work. Her sleeves are rolled, water dripping from the basin.

"Good morrow, maidens. We thought you should know," I say, stepping forward, "that we're going into the woods along the ridge, to see if we can bring in more food."

Henry adds, "Aye. We thought we could see what game we could find."

Alyssa nods, setting down her dish carefully. "The children are getting better," she says. "They've gone back to sleep after eating their breakfast. They need their rest." She glances at Danielle. "We'll go with you. We can help."

I raise an eyebrow, surprised. "You're certain? The trail and the woods make for rough travel."

Alyssa smiles, her green eyes sparkling. "We can manage. We'll keep up."

Henry grins. "Well, we can't argue with that. Seems we'll have more hands than we expected."

Before we set off, Alyssa holds up a hand. "We should tell Goody Tinker. She ought to know where we're going, and she can keep an eye on the children while we're gone."

I nod. "Aye. Best we do that."

The four of us walk to the Tinkers' cabin. Goodwife Tinker answers her front door, and we explain our mission and ask our favor. After she agrees to look in on the children once in a while, we set out toward the forest.

The hunt awaits, and with these women beside us, I feel we are stronger and more capable than ever. We move quietly through the trees, our eyes sharp, looking for any sign of game. Henry and I each carry a musket, ready to aim should a deer or other creature appear before us.

Alyssa crouches beside a large patch of soil where the dead grass is crushed. "Do you see this?" she whispers. "A doe rested here not long ago. A buck will often come along and mark his territory over the spots where the doe lies down. In fact, I can smell this territory has already been marked."

Henry frowns. "Mark their territory? Whatever do you mean? Mark it with what?"

"With urine," Danielle says, giggling.

I have to force back a laugh at that. "You mean the male deer actually urinates where the female was lying?" I ask, incredulous.

Alyssa smiles. "That's right. My grandfather taught me all about how to track deer. You can follow the scent if you recognize the odor. Most hunters miss it."

Henry shakes his head in disbelief. "By the Lord, that's clever."

We follow the trail she indicates, careful not to disturb the leaves. After a few moments, a young buck emerges into a small clearing, unaware of our presence. Alyssa signals us to stay low. "Aim just behind the shoulder. Don't rush. Wait for the beast to steady his breathing."

I raise my musket, take a careful breath, and fire. The buck is hit, but bolts, runs a few paces, and then collapses.

"Well done, Owens!" Henry says, clapping me on the shoulder. "A clean shot. That'll feed the village."

I shake my head, looking to the women. "If it weren't for you two, I wouldn't have managed it at all. This is as much your victory as mine."

We approach the large animal, and Henry grips one leg. "It'll take all four of us to carry this massive fellow."

We strain together, carrying the deer along the leafy path. Step by step, we make our way toward the village to hang and clean the deer.

When we return, we find a sturdy branch between two maple trees and secure the animal, its legs tied to keep it steady. I hand

Alyssa my extra knife, and Danielle and Henry get started gathering brush and logs for a fire.

We're well into our work when voices drift from the path, and I glance up to see Governor Bradford, Captain Standish, Samuel Tinker, and, predictably, Priscilla Mullins with her cluster of followers. Behind them walks John Alden, a barrel maker, his eyes wary but curious. None speaks at first. They only stand there, watching as we work.

Henry shakes his head at the deer, wiping sweat from his forehead. "This is a massive creature. We may as well make a scrap pile," he says. "There'll always be bits you can't use."

Alyssa looks up sharply. "Scrap pile?" she repeats. "No need for a scrap pile. Every part of this deer will be put to use."

Danielle picks up a clean bone and taps it like a drum. "Even the marrow, if boiled, feeds the village. Nothing is wasted. We can use it for bone broth, which is highly nutritious or can be used as salves for dry skin and chapped lips."

Young Samuel Tinker leans in, curiosity winning over caution. "You can use all of it?"

Alyssa nods. "The meat feeds us, naturally. Bones become broth, salve, tools, needles, hooks, and awls. Sinews braid into thread for sewing or bowstrings. Fat renders into tallow for lamps or cooking. The hide, once scraped and tanned, makes clothing, straps, even bags for carrying goods. Every part of this blessed animal serves a purpose, and we should be thanking God for His grace and presence in this animal."

Bradford steps closer, his eyes bright. "These are practical uses I had not fully considered. Your knowledge of such things is nothing short of astonishing, Mistress Montgomery, Mistress Whitman."

Standish's hand rests on the hilt of his sword, but his tone carries approval. "Aye. Such understanding strengthens the village. We are wise to learn from you."

Priscilla Mullins flushes, her voice shrill. "How can you make such remarks, Captain Standish? Do the scriptures themselves not say that we should not suffer women to teach men? It's savagery! It's witchcraft! Women should be in the kitchen, meekness our veil. How dare these two be out here hacking at carcasses, and worse, teaching men! This is unacceptable!"

A few of her followers nod, whispering in agreement. John Adler crosses his arms; his expression tells me he agrees.

Henry steps forward, his fists clenched. "These maidens did this for the children! Those who lost parents yesterday would have nothing if we had waited. This is care, not witchcraft."

I add, "Mistress Montgomery and Mistress Whitman have been nothing but thoughtful, kind, and hard-working since they arrived. If anything, they are blessings from God."

Priscilla stamps her foot. "They should be thrown out! Banished! Governor Bradford, do something!"

Mistress Whitman meets her glare evenly. "We seek only to help. That is all."

Samuel Tinker clears his throat. "She's right. We'd starve without their work."

Bradford raises a hand before Priscilla to still her. "We will not banish those who act for the good of the village. They teach, provide, and care. That is worth more than idle complaint."

Standish glances at the deer and then at the women. "Show us how we can help."

I step back for a moment, wiping blood from my hands, and watch those who offer a hand move from the carcass to the fire.

Alyssa's eyes are filled with determination. She's clever, brave, kind, and so capable. How is it possible that such women exist, that they are here, with us, not asking for praise, not seeking reward, just giving all they can to help?

I've seen courage before, yes, in men and boys in the woods or on the sea, but this is something else entirely. This is a strength that demands respect, that draws others to it, and yet, beneath it, there is laughter, warmth, care, beauty, and grace. They think of the children, of the village, of all of us, and they do it without a thought for themselves.

I look around at the small group helping, the fire crackling, the smell of roasting venison filling the air. For a moment, everything is right. I want to tell Alyssa how much she means, how remarkable she is, but words fail me. What could I say that would capture even a fraction of my admiration?

And then the thought strikes, bitter and sharp: half the village still wishes them gone. Priscilla Mullins and her gossipy sort will never stop scheming, never stop whispering. Will Alyssa and Danielle stay? Will they tolerate this place, these people, the constant friction? My heart hopes that they will. My mind fears they won't.

I watch them laugh quietly together, sharing a jest, sharing work, and I hope against hope that they remain, that they allow themselves to belong here, with us, despite the odds.

Alas, the world is harsh, and I know better than to expect miracles.

RESCUED

Alyssa

THE FIRE HAS DWINDLED TO A LOW, AMBER GLOW, BARELY LIGHTING THE walls of the cabin. Outside, the trees sway, their shadows stretching across the clearing like long, spooky fingers. The children lie asleep, tucked beneath quilts. I sink onto a bed beside Danielle, my arms hugging my knees, and let the quiet press in.

"These people," I murmur, staring at the fading embers. "They remind me of what will happen in Salem. They're far too rigid, fearful, and ready to punish any woman who steps beyond her place. Just a few decades from now, villagers like these will hang women for less than what we've said and done."

Danielle's gaze meets mine, dark and thoughtful. "I know," she says quietly. "It's chilling. Their piety is so strict, so absolute, it borders on superstition. I can see how fear runs through them already, how quickly it takes hold."

I nod, thinking of the contrast between how Danielle and I grew up in church and this. My parents took us every Sunday and taught us to pray, read scripture, and to honor God, but never like this, not with judgment hanging over every act. We were taught faith as guidance, not a cudgel to strike fear into others.

"I miss my family," I whisper. "I want to go back to them."

Danielle's hand finds mine. "I understand," she says. "But we're here now. I feel as if we were sent for a purpose. I don't have a family that even knows I exist, not really, but… I understand. If we can find a way back to the future, I'll go with you—no matter what."

I squeeze her hand, heart tightening. "Thank you for understanding. Tomorrow, we'll try the ocean," I murmur. "Maybe it will carry us home to 2025."

Danielle shrugs. "Whatever happens, we'll face it together. If the water won't take us home, then we survive here, together."

I lean back on the bed, letting the warmth of the fire seep in, yet a chill runs through me at the thoughts of the villagers turning dangerous. Half of them already whisper and already judge.

Sleep tugs at my eyelids, but my mind races. I imagine the ocean, dark and endless. I remember the way the waves pulled and twisted. I imagine returning to a world that is ours—or dying trying. My chest tightens with the risk, but with Danielle beside me, I always feel stronger and braver.

I close my eyes, clutching the thin blanket to my chest. Tomorrow, time may decide everything for itself, and I hope against hope that we both make it back to the future.

The next morning, before rising from bed to prepare breakfast, I say a prayer. I pray for the village, for the leaders, men, women, and children. I pray for Henry and Isaac. Then, I ask God to help Danielle and me return home safely.

Danielle scrubs the last of the venison and squash from the plates, and I rinse them carefully. The children are fed, their small bellies warm, their cheeks flushed with health again.

"Should we tell Henry and Isaac we're leaving?" Danielle asks.

"No. I don't think we should. They wouldn't understand, and they'd try to stop us. We can't tell them the truth —that we're from another time. They'd never be able to believe us."

Danielle leans against the table, drying her hands on a towel. "I know you're right. I hate it, but it's safer this way. We'll leave without goodbyes."

Her eyes brim with tears, and I lean over and give her a hug. "I know you have feelings for Henry. I'm beginning to have feelings for Isaac myself, but we can't risk it." Not to mention the children, but at least they are healthy now.

Danielle sniffles and nods, and we finish the last dishes in silence, stacking them carefully, making sure the cabin is neat.

I glance toward the children. "We should ask Goody Tinker to watch them. They're much healthier now, and she'll know what to do after what we showed her about the mushrooms."

Danielle nods, and we tell the children we're going to fetch Goody Tinker to look after them.

When we find ourselves back on the beach, the sea stretches before us, deep and dark, the waves rolling and crashing in endless rhythm. Danielle slips her hand into mine. "Should we pray?"

I bow my head, asking for guidance, for safety, for courage. The wind whips my hair, the salt stings my eyes, and the horizon trembles with the promise of the unknown. Being here has strengthened my faith, despite my not even realizing that I'd drifted away.

We step into the water, each wave curling around our ankles, then knees, then thighs. The sand drops away beneath us as we swim further, our hands gripping each other's. The shallow turns to deep almost without notice, and the currents tug at us, playful yet insistent.

The roar of the ocean grows, waves crashing over our shoulders, tossing us with a force that makes my heart lurch. I swallow hard, tasting salt on my lips, letting the pull of the ocean carry me outward. The world behind us, the children, the cabins, Henry, Isaac… shrinks to a memory. All that exists is the fragile hope that this water will take us home.

Salt stings my eyes, my lungs burn, and every stroke feels like wading through lead. Danielle is beside me, coughing, her hand slicing the water, but the waves are relentless, crashing over us in heavy, cold swells. My fingers claw at the surface. The deep blue yawns beneath us, swallowing all sense of direction. I try to think of home, but each wave knocks the breath from my lungs. Panic surges through me. I can't keep my head above water, and can't tell if Danielle is still breathing either.

Then, a strong hand grips my wrist. Another pulls at my arm. The motion is quick and urgent, guiding me up through the heavy water. I kick and grab, my lungs gasping, my heart hammering.

Danielle's voice breaks through, ragged and scared, but full of relief. "Someone's helping us!"

"Oh, thank God—the Coast Guard!" I gasp, relief flooding me. My mind flashes to the crash, the car spinning on the highway as we plunged into the ocean. "We made be back in 2025! The Coast Guard has come to rescue us from the wreck!"

Then I'm lifted into a narrow wooden boat, oars dipping rhythmically in the waves, and the truth hits: this is no Coast Guard.

Danielle is hauled up next, her teeth chattering, her hair plastered to her face. I reach out instinctively, squeezing her. She collapses beside me in the narrow boat. Water drips from our sleeves and hair, soaking the planks beneath us. We huddle together, shivering, our arms wrapped around each other, our eyes wide as the men maneuver the boat closer to the shore.

Each wave rocks us violently, and I watch in awe as they leap from the sand into the surf, guiding the boat. Their strong hands grip the sides until the craft bumps onto the shallow sand. We clamber out, our feet sinking into the wet grains, cold and unforgiving, and I can hardly believe we are alive.

Danielle falls beside me, trembling but all right, sputtering out a prayer in thanks. I clasp my hands together, my chest heaving, and join her. I don't know who these people are, but their skill and strength have saved us from the dark, endless ocean. The roar of the surf still fills my ears, but the panic slowly recedes, leaving exhaustion in its place.

A figure steps forward, tall, handsome, and radiating calm authority. He lifts a hand in greeting, his eyes bright and friendly. The others gather behind him, their voices carrying in a strange, musical cadence. I have never heard this language before, yet the tone is gentle.

Finally, the man speaks directly to us, slowing his words so we might understand. "I am Samoset," he says, pointing to himself, then to the others around him as he says other names.

The realization hits, the weight of it settling in my chest. We have not been rescued by just anyone. We are in the hands of someone remarkable, someone who commands respect among his people—and from history.

Danielle and I huddle together, keeping our voices low, barely above a breath. "Do you realize… this is him?" I murmur, glancing quickly at Samoset as he turns to speak with the others. "The same Samoset we read about, and now he's right here."

Danielle steps forward, a huge smile beaming from her face. "I'm just… I'm a huge fan."

Samoset tilts his head, his eyes narrowing slightly. "A huge fan?" he asks, each word coming out as an individual thought.

Danielle blushes but keeps her composure. "Oh, it's just that we've heard of you, and we really appreciate your work."

He inclines his head slowly, his expression calm but intrigued, a faint smile tugging at his lips. "Do you wish to meet my people?" he asks, his voice kind and confident. "They are close by, and they will welcome you."

I exchange a glance with Danielle, and her eyes mirror my own stunned amazement. After everything, the ocean, the fear, the freezing waves, each new moment in this place feels impossible.

"We would be honored," I manage to say, my voice trembling. "And thank you for rescuing us."

Danielle chimes in. "Yes. We appreciate your help very much. Thank you."

Samoset nods. "Follow me."

We do, trudging across wet sand into the forest. As we round a bend, the woods open onto a clearing where a small village rests in quiet harmony. Bark-and-wood structures cluster around a central fire. The smell of roasting fish drifts toward us.

Samoset pauses and gestures for us to wait and then introduces us to the group. "These are my people," he says. "They live here, care for one another, teach, provide. You are welcome here."

I can barely speak. The village is alive with purpose. Women tend small gardens of corn, beans, and squash. Children chase each other around the open space, laughing and shrieking. Men craft tools and weave nets, while elders sit quietly, checking the cooking fires or shaping clay pots. Every movement feels deliberate, full of cheerful intent.

Danielle whispers, just loud enough for me to hear, "Alyssa... can you believe this? We're really meeting them. We've taught about these people. We've re-enacted their lives, but I never imagined we'd meet them."

I nod, my chest tight with wonder, soaking it all in. Somehow, amid fear and uncertainty, hope takes root in my heart. Here, in the presence of Samoset and his people, we glimpse a world in balance, a life lived fully in harmony with the earth.

KIEHTAN WATCHES OVER ALL

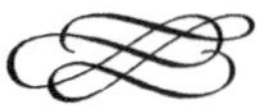

Isaac

Dawn's dewy fog clings to the trees as I make my way toward the shoreline, the sand damp beneath my boots. The bay stretches before us, a silver-gray mirror beneath the rising sun. I spot Henry already at the edge of the water, dragging the small rowboat into the shallows. He looks up when I approach, his expression brightening, but there's an edge of concern in his eyes that mirrors my own.

"Good morrow, Lewis," I call. "Ready to see if these new nets hold their weight?"

He smiles. "Aye, but where are our fair companions, Owens?"

"I went to the Connor house first," I say, pushing the boat deeper into the water. "Goody Tinker's there, but the maidens aren't. She said they asked her to watch over the children, but she doesn't know where they went."

Henry's grin vanishes. He scratches the back of his neck. "They told no one whither they went?"

"No," I reply. "There's been no sign of them at all, which isn't like them, Henry. I—" My voice falters, and I bite my lip. "I'm worried about them. I've never felt like this before about anyone."

Henry's gaze drops to the water, his hand on the side of the boat. "Aye. I can't stop thinking about Danielle. She's clever, brave, everything a man could hope for. I hate the thought of something happening to them."

I nod, gripping the oar. "You don't think they went searching for the others from their shipwreck, do you?"

Henry and I jump into the boat just as the current picks up. "I hope not. Certainly, they wouldn't go anywhere without telling us farewell."

I check the net we brought. The weave is tight and strong. "Aye. I should think not. Surely we have at the very least earned a farewell."

I drop the net over the side, watching it sink, weighted carefully with stones. The rhythm of the water soothes me, yet my mind keeps returning to the women. Where could they have gone?

We fish the morning away, nets drifting, lines snapping taut, the occasional catch filling the boat with silver flashes. Still, every look toward the shore carries the same gnawing thought. Alyssa and Danielle are somewhere beyond reach, and all we can do is haul our catch and pray they come to no harm.

By the time the sun hangs high, our haul is respectable, but my heart remains uneasy. Henry notices my glances toward the trees. "Isaac," he says, "Shall we try to track them?"

I nod. "Aye. I thought I could put the worry out of my mind, but it's not dissipating."

Even as we row back to shore with the fish, my mind drifts to the maidens and where fate has carried them this morning.

We tug the rowboat onto the wet sand, water sloshing around our boots, and stretch our cramped muscles. We're at least a league and a half away from where we started.

Henry rubs his shoulders, but his eyes are sharp, scanning the shoreline. "If they wandered, we shall find them, but we are awfully far away from the village now. Shall we head back?"

I nod. Just then, I notice the sand is dotted with footprints, fresh from the morning mist drying over the bay. I crouch, squinting at the impressions. There are many outlines of men's boots, bare feet, and smaller ones, delicate, clearly belonging to women. Two sets lead into the forest, weaving between dune grass and scrub. Mixed among them are broader prints.

"Do you see?" I point them out to Henry. "Here, these small prints could be from their boots."

"Then they're not alone. Someone's most assuredly with them. We must be careful."

Abandoning the fish for now, we follow the trail, moving carefully, leaving the sand behind and stepping onto pine needles and fallen leaves. The tracks lead us deeper, the sand fading into the forest floor, the prints more distinct in the soft soil.

Eventually, the trees part, and we glimpse a clearing ahead. Figures move near the center, a small group of people. Henry and I are still for a moment, unsure, but then we relax as the men nearest spot us in the tree, and their expressions prove calm and welcoming.

One of the men steps forward, his hand raised in greeting. I mimic the gesture. "We... we're looking for two maidens," I say carefully, pointing toward the group.

He tilts his head, speaking in a melodic, unfamiliar tongue. Another man steps forward and gestures for us to follow. There's no hostility, only a guiding patience. We tread carefully, and soon, Alyssa and Danielle come into view. Relief floods me, and I quicken my pace.

Danielle spins around when Henry calls her name. She grins, waving, and Alyssa joins her. The women look exhausted but unharmed, standing beside a tall man with calm authority.

"This is Samoset," Alyssa says quickly, gesturing to him. "He speaks English. He learned it from English traders. He's originally from much further north, and from a different tribe, but he's here with this group now, helping them."

Samoset inclines his head toward us, his eyes warm. "You are welcome here," he says in perfect English.

Henry and I introduce ourselves, words spilling out awkwardly.

"I'm Isaac Owens," I say. "This is Henry Lewis. Thank you for your hospitality."

Samoset nods and gestures to the clearing. The village around us is alive with motion. People tend gardens, repair shelters, and prepare food. Others gather near, curious, keeping their eyes on us.

Samoset leads us across the clearing, past children darting between the huts and adults bent over their daily tasks. Everything moves with purpose, the men checking fish drying on racks, women braiding mats and shaping clay pots.

"We live completely within the rhythm of the land," he murmurs. "Every motion has meaning."

Ahead, Samoset gestures to a larger, more ornate hut. "This is our sachem, Massasoit Ousamequin, he says, his voice calm. "He will welcome you."

We walk inside of the hut. Massasoit Ousamequin's voice rises, low and resonant, each syllable deliberate, carrying a cadence that seems to flow from the earth itself. The words are foreign, but there's a warmth and depth in them, like a prayer whispered over the wind and waters. Even without understanding, I feel a solemn blessing threaded through his speech, a sense that he is acknowledging our presence as part of a larger harmony.

Samoset leans closer, translating. "He says the Great Spirit, Kiehtan, watches over all who walk here. He honors your journey and offers you protection while you are in his land."

I bow my head slightly, awed. There is a calm authority in Massasoit, a spiritual gravity that makes the cabin, the people, and even the ocean outside feel connected in a way I can scarcely describe. To be here, in the presence of such a man, is humbling. Since Alyssa and Danielle introduced us to the women with the vegetables, I've come to realize how wrong I was about the people who have lived here for so long.

I nod at Massasoit Ousamequin again, offering a quiet word of thanks. He inclines his, a deliberate motion, and then gestures toward the doorway. Without fanfare, Henry and I step back, letting the chief return to his meditation.

Outside, the air is crisp, the scent of smoke and cooking drifting from the village, and we fall into step toward the open clearing where Alyssa and Danielle are already watching the women at their weaving.

We observe the Indians nearly all day, taking in every detail of how they live, how they provide for one another, how they tend the fires and gardens, and I feel a quiet respect growing in my chest. But the sun is dipping low now, and I glance at the others.

"Best we head back," I say. "It wouldn't do to be walking after dark."

We approach Samoset to bid him farewell and thank him again. "We hope to visit again," I say. Henry, Alyssa, and Danielle add their own words of thanks, and Samoset nods.

Others step forward, each offering us a heaping basket of corn, beans, and dried fish, their hands strong and sure as they place them in our arms. The weight is generous, a tangible gift of their care and goodwill. Alyssa and Danielle grin at one another, marveling at the bounty, and I feel a deep sense of gratitude for their generosity as we turn to retrace our steps back to Plymouth.

When we step back onto the sand to retrieve the fish we caught earlier, our hearts are as full as our baskets. The voices of the people, the smell of roasting fish and fresh herbs, the laughter of children all linger. I carry it with me, a memory of discipline, community, and care, as tangible as the sustenance in my arms.

Alyssa walks beside me along the worn forest path back to Plymouth. The air is cool with evening mist. Henry and Danielle are far enough ahead with their laughter and chatter lost to the distance, leaving just the two of us. I find myself stealing glances at Alyssa. Her beauty is unmatched even by nature itself.

"This meeting with Samoset and his people," she says. "It could change things for Plymouth, for all of us."

"Aye," I reply, nodding. "Knowing the Indians, learning from them, it could be the difference between survival and hardship. They have knowledge of the land, the waters, and their ways could guide us."

"Actually," she says. "They aren't Indians."

"What do you mean?" I ask. "Certainly you weren't about to refer to them as savages. I know you better than that by now."

"Of course not, but they are not Indians. Christopher Columbus made a mistake when he called them Indians. After all, we are not in India, are we?"

"Aye. We certainly aren't in India. So what is the name of the people?"

"Well, Samoset is from a people called the Abenaki from many days' journey north of here. And Massasoit Ousamequin is the chief, kind of like a king, of the Wampanoag people. In fact, most of our people would probably think his name is Massasoit, but that just means he's their sachem, or their leader. His name is actually Ousamequin."

"It's strange how much miscommunication can occur when people aren't truly trying to understand one another," I say. "And what if we were to call them Indians?"

"We'd sound as foolish as Columbus, and they'd have no idea what you were referring to." Alyssa laughs.

"How could you know such things? How do you seem to know all about this new world?"

"I pay attention and ask questions," she says. And I certainly believe her.

She looks up at me, and for a moment, it feels like more than just conversation passes between us. I want to reach out, to hold her hand fully, perhaps even draw her closer, but such desires are dangerous. My faith teaches restraint, modesty, the separation of hearts until proper bonds are made. Yet, the pull is undeniable, a longing I can't fully suppress.

"I never thought I'd see such skill, such harmony with one another and the earth," Alyssa murmurs.

"Aye," I answer, my voice low. "And it is a blessing that they welcomed us. We must honor and protect their guidance and friendship."

When we reach the Connor house, Henry shoulders open the

door. Goody Tinker greets us, rising at once from her stool. Her eyes grow with curiosity at the size of our bounty.

"Mercy, what abundance!" she exclaims, bustling forward, her hands moving from basket to basket as though she can't believe her eyes. "Such fish, such corn, such beans! Bless the Lord for His provision!" She clucks her tongue, delighted, and sets to making space on the table, fussing over how best to store it all.

Alyssa and Danielle laugh as they carry their baskets in, their clothing damp with the day's work, their hair loose around their faces. The children, stirred from play, crowd near, their eyes shining. Already, Alyssa has a pan in hand, her movements brisk and sure, laying out some of the fish the Abenaki gave us to fry for their supper. The sound of it simmering fills the room, and a warmth spreads through me that is more than firelight.

I stand back, watching the glow on her face as she bends over the pan. For the first time, I believe our people may endure here. And for the first time, I admit to myself the quiet truth: my hope is not only for Plymouth, but for Alyssa.

I bow my head, murmuring a prayer of thanks, though my heart beats with a yearning I dare not name aloud.

JUST THE TWO OF US

Alyssa

I watch the Connor children at the breakfast table, their laughter spilling over the bowls of oats and berries. Their cheeks are rosy, and their eyes are bright, both welcome signs of how much stronger they've grown. As Danielle and I pass around apple slices, I catch little Sarah Connor sneaking a second before her brother even finishes his first. Their faces look rounder this morning, a faint flush replacing the sallow gray that had haunted them since we first arrived. I never thought I'd feel relief at something so simple as seeing children eat, but here, in this world, survival is a blessing.

"They're getting stronger already," Danielle whispers, settling beside me with a satisfied smile. "It's amazing what steady nutrition can do."

I nod, brushing a strand of hair out of my eyes. "Yes. I was just thinking the same thing. I didn't think we'd be coming back here to see them at all. I thought we'd be back home by now." My voice comes out shakier than I mean for it to. Memories from yesterday won't leave me—the cold rush of water filling my lungs when we tried to go back, thinking the ocean would return us home. Instead of ending up in 2025, we nearly drowned. My chest aches just remembering it.

Danielle doesn't flinch. She squeezes my wrist as if to anchor me. "Maybe we were meant to stay. I mean, come on, Alyssa, meeting Samoset and his people? That doesn't feel like an accident. It feels like fate."

"You mean you feel like we are supposed to be the ones who start the dialogue with the indigenous people here?"

"We already have. Everything we've ever learned about this area, the land we grew up on, we have just become the first representatives of our people with the Wampanoag people."

"I guess you're right, but it doesn't change the fact that I desperately miss my parents, my brother, and my sister. I miss our students. I miss our old lives, Danielle."

Her eyes soften. "I know. I do, too. But maybe our mission is here. Maybe saving lives now is what we're meant to do. Look at these children. Look at them smiling. What if this is why we were brought back?"

I shake my head, though the words stick in my throat. I want to believe her, but the ache for my family, our own time, is a raw wound. "You might be ready to stay forever, but I'm not."

Danielle's smile shifts, something sly sparking in her eyes. "Not even for Isaac?"

Heat creeps up my neck. "What are you talking about?"

"I see the way you look at him and the way he looks at you," she says, her tone teasing but gentle. "Don't deny it. You're falling for him harder than you ever expected."

I can't deny it—the way Isaac's gaze lingers on me, the way he listens as though my words matter, even when I feel like I'm unraveling here. "I am," I admit in a whisper.

Danielle leans closer, her voice low. "Then maybe you should spend time with him, away from all this noise. Go on a walk. Or better yet, go foraging with him, just the two of you. Then you'll know if what you feel is real or just survival binding you together."

I glance at the Connor children and then toward the door where sunlight spills across the threshold. I feel butterflies in my stomach at the thought of being alone with Isaac, and testing whatever is building between us.

"I think you're right," I say. "I think I'll go find him."

Danielle gives me a wink, hands me a basket, spins me around, and uses both hands on my bottom to shove me toward the front door.

The Connor children's laughter trails behind me when I step outside. The village is alive with morning work: women spreading laundry to dry, men moving barrels of supplies, voices calling back and forth. I walk to Isaac's house and spot him in the yard.

He stands gripping an axe, splitting logs in clean, powerful strokes. His shirt is unlaced at the neck, and he's damp from sweat across his chest and shoulders. Each time he swings, the muscles in his forearms flex, the motion sure and unhurried, as though strength is as natural to him as breath.

My feet slow without my permission. Sunlight glances off his face, carving out the strong line of his jaw, the sculpted edge of his cheekbones. His dark hair falls loose around his temples, a strand clinging to his skin.

I should look away, but I don't.

As if sensing me, he straightens and turns. His eyes catch mine, and for a moment, neither of us moves. Then, a faint, knowing smile touches his mouth.

"Good morrow, Mistress Montgomery." His deep voice carries across the space.

"Good morning." My fingers tighten on the basket's handle. "I was wondering, would you like to take a stroll with me? We might find something useful to bring back." I know it's unusual for a single man and a single woman to be left alone together, but we will be doing something useful for the village.

He sets the axe aside at once, wiping his palms on his trousers. "Aye. That would please me." Crossing the yard, he takes a basket from the pile by his door and strolls toward me.

We leave the houses behind and step beneath the trees, where the hush of the forest envelopes us. Every brush of his shoulder against mine sparks heat low in my stomach.

"It is strange," he says finally, "how we met Samoset, and that his people were so open, welcoming, and free spirited."

I nod. "It was wondrous, and certainly an honor to meet them. What is strange?"

"Just how you spoke with them as though it were the simplest thing. I have never known a woman to carry herself with such confidence and poise."

My cheeks burn. "I appreciate your kind words. I simply try to be kind to everyone."

"That is what I mean," he says, halting near a thicket of berries. He doesn't bend to gather them. Instead, he looks into my eyes. "You see the world with love, Alyssa. You put others first, and it's a trait I find most appealing."

Before I can answer, his hand grazes mine on the basket's rim, tentative. I let my fingers slip into his, and he leans down.

Isaac's lips brush mine, warm, gentle, and questioning. The kiss is brief, but it leaves me dizzy, every part of me wanting more of him. When he pulls back, his eyes search mine, and I know he feels it, too.

For the first time since I stumbled into this impossible world, I see myself staying.

The afternoon slips away in a blur of green leaves and sunlight. Isaac and I wander deeper into the forest, our baskets gradually filling with bright berries, wild onions, and nuts shaken down from the trees. We find a patch of wild grapevines twining close to the ground, their blossoms fading but the fruit still firm. I show him how to pick them from the stem without harming the plant, his hands brushing mine in ways that make my skin tingle.

It is easy to forget the world when it is just the two of us. We talk of little things like the children in the village, the changing season, the way the air sharpens in early autumn, and yet beneath every word is a current pulling us closer. We laugh, fall into comfortable silence, and sometimes he simply looks at me as though I am something miraculous he never expected to find.

And yes, we kiss again more than once. At first, it is tentative and sweet, then bolder, lingering, and every time his lips touch mine, the knot of longing for home inside me loosens. With him, I feel safe, seen, and wanted. It's strange that he is willing to go against his beliefs to kiss me, but I suppose he must feel this primal urge deep within him that has been pulling at me since the moment his hand first touched mine.

By the time we turn back toward the village, our baskets are heavy, and my heart is heavier still with swirling emotions, new romance mixing with yearning for familiarity.

When the houses come into view, I feel the day's spell break. Isaac shifts the basket higher on his arm, his face carefully composed, though his eyes still carry that quiet heat. He leads the way back to the square, where voices and laughter rise again, the safety of privacy gone.

We stop at the edge of the common. I clutch my basket tighter, reluctant to let the moment end. His hand grazes mine as though he, too, is unwilling to part. Our eyes meet, our bodies buzzing with the unspoken wish to kiss again, but there are people watching, and we both know we can't risk being seen for piety's sake. If they're calling me a witch for feeding children healthy meals, I can't imagine what they'd say if I kissed a man I'm not married to in broad daylight.

"Until later," Isaac says, and though the words are simple, they warm me all the way through. He heads off toward the villagers to share what we gathered, while I carry my share back to the Connor house.

Inside, Danielle is sitting by the hearth with one of the children in her lap. She looks up when she sees me, and I know my flushed cheeks and bright eyes have betrayed me.

"Well?" she asks, her grin already wide.

I bite my lip, but it is no use. I whisper to her, "We kissed."

Her squeal makes the kids giggle, though they have no idea why. Danielle claps her hands over her mouth, her eyes dancing. "I knew it! Tell me everything."

We fall into giddy whispers like schoolgirls, even though we are grown women who should be more sophisticated. She teases me about his buff arms, about the way he watches me. I laugh and confess more than I mean to, my heart racing just to remember the feel of his lips on mine.

But when her laughter fades, the gravity of my thoughts presses in. I still miss my family. I want my own time, my own life back. The grief of losing it gnaws at me.

And yet, there is Isaac. His handsome face, sexy physique, his gentle, comforting words, and the way he makes me feel as though I belong here with him.

If I stay, I risk losing everything. If I leave, assuming I can, I will lose him, and I don't know which ache is worse.

LONGING

I KISSED HER.

Alyssa Montgomery. Yesterday, when no one was near, when words faltered and my resolve broke, I touched her hand, then her cheek, and before I could command myself otherwise, I leaned close and pressed my lips to hers. The memory burns hotter than any fire.

I ought to feel nothing but shame. A godly man doesn't act with such haste, nor does he take liberties with a woman who is not his wife. Last night, I prayed for forgiveness, begged the Lord to rid me of this weakness, and yet, I don't truly feel that it was a sin.

I can't tell if I erred against Heaven or if Heaven itself guided me to her. That is the torment, and the reason that even as I feel the sting of guilt, I want to kiss her again. I want to feel her bare skin against mine….

Henry's voice interrupts my thoughts as he falls into step next to me. "A pleasant morrow," he says, glancing at the rising sun.

"Aye. The forest is alive with sound. It will make the journey easier."

We stop before the Connor dwelling, and my heart beats faster as I lift my hand to knock. Before I can, the door creaks open, and Danielle appears, her cap tugged low over her curls, her eyes dancing with mischief.

"Well, look at you two," she says. "Bright eyed and ready for the day."

Henry clears his throat. "You look well this morning, Mistress Whitman."

"We came to ask if you would join us," I say. "We're going to the place where we first met Samoset. Perhaps we will meet him again or others of his tribe. We thought you might like to join us."

Danielle smirks. "We'd love to go with you. Thank you for inviting us."

When Alyssa steps into view, my heart gives a foolish leap. She gathers her shawl close, her eyes searching mine just long enough to weaken my knees. "Where would we love to go?" she asks with a playful grin.

"Good morrow, Mistress Montgomery," I answer, my throat dry. "We were thinking of joining the Wampanoag again today, if they'll welcome us."

"Of course we'll come," she says without hesitation.

After making arrangements for the children, the four of us stroll down the path, the village falling away behind. Autumn leaves crunch beneath our boots, the air alive with the rustle of branches and the calls of birds. My thoughts war between prayer and lustful memories, between God's law and the taste of Alyssa's lips.

We push through a tangle of oaks and maples, and I keep my eyes sharp. The forest smells of damp earth and smoke from distant fires. "Samoset must be out here somewhere," I say.

Henry moves ahead, scanning the brush. "I think I saw smoke near the creek," he says.

Alyssa halts mid-step, raising a finger toward a bend in the stream. "There—by the water," she whispers.

Kneeling on the bank, Samoset is showing two young boys how to dip their nets into the current, lifting small fish carefully from the water. Their laughter rings through the trees as he guides them with patience.

Samoset glances up, nods, and waves for us to come closer. "You've found me," he says, his voice calm. "The stream has been generous this morning."

As we approach, another man moves through the trees behind him, carrying a bundle of dried reeds and furs. Samoset gestures toward him. "This is Tisquantum," he says. "He has come to help me today."

I introduce the four of us to Tisquantum as Alyssa and Danielle whisper to each other, giggling, which I find odd. They've never been rude before. Perhaps they're simply nervous.

"It's an honor to meet you, Tisquantum," Danielle says with a smile spreading from each ear.

"Big fan?" Samoset asks.

"Big fan. Huge," she replies.

"Forgive my friend again. She has just really appreciated what you have done for the village. We all have," Alyssa says in her graceful, elegant manner.

A few steps beyond, a woman tends a small fire, grinding roots and herbs with practiced hands. Samoset points to her. "She is Obbatinewat's sister, Kesuk. They're both healers. She prepares what the people need."

I watch as she mixes powders into a small clay pot. The smell is sharp, clean, and I can tell the herbs are chosen with care. I glance at Alyssa. Her eyes widen, admiration and respect mirrored in Danielle's gaze as well.

Samoset straightens, looking at us. "Did you come seeking more food?"

I step forward. "Ah, no, but we do thank you for the food you blessed us with before. We did come to ask you if next time we may bring our leaders. We'd like to introduce our Governor Bradford and Captain Standish to your chief, only if he welcomes the idea."

"I can't say. That is for our leader to decide. Come, and we will ask him together."

Samoset leads us along familiar paths, Tisquantum at his side, until we reach the hut where we met their king before.

Samoset speaks with Massasoit Ousamequin, and after he explains our request, the leader nods his head and speaks to Samoset.

Samoset translates his response. "Massasoit Ousamequin says you are welcome. Your leaders may come. We will meet them, and the meeting will be good."

After our meeting, the healer woman appears from the edge of the clearing. In her hands is a basket overflowing with bundles of dried herbs, roots, and small pouches of leaves. She approaches Alyssa and Danielle slowly, bowing slightly, her face worn, and yet, serene.

"For you," she says in forced English, holding the basket out.

Alyssa steps forward, taking it carefully. "Thank you," she says.

Danielle gives the woman a warm embrace that seems to perplex her at first, but in the end, she relaxes into Danielle's arms.

"We appreciate your generosity," Alyssa adds.

"What do you suppose all this is for?" Danielle whispers once the woman steps back into the forest.

Alyssa peers inside, gently lifting a bundle of dried leaves. "Some of these are teas, I think. There's sage, mint… oh, and echinacea." She lifts a small vial filled with a dark liquid. "Tinctures, maybe for fevers or wounds."

Danielle runs her fingers over a bundle of roots. "These must be for poultices. Look at the bark. It's harsh on its own, but mixed with something, it'll draw out infection."

"These will be so useful during the winter," Alyssa says, smiling faintly at me. "Coughs, colds, cuts… even stomach troubles, I think."

I nod, trying to sound thoughtful. "They think ahead. They know the cold months will be hard. It's so kind of them to prepare for us as friends."

I hoist the basket onto my shoulder, careful not to crush the contents, and begin the walk back to Plymouth. The forest is quiet, debris crunching underfoot, the sun slanting through the branches like gold. I steal a glance at Alyssa, her beautiful face radiating femininity, and I must resist the pull I feel toward her.

By the time we reach the settlement, Governor Bradford and Captain Standish are waiting, along with a few other settlers. They eye the basket with curiosity, and I can see the skepticism lingering on some of the faces around us.

"We spent the day with Massasoit Ousamequin and his people," I say. "We asked if it would be a welcome meeting between the two leaders, ours and theirs."

Standish nods, his arms crossed. "Did you now, Owens? And what was the reply?"

"They welcome us all. Their leader said it would be a good meeting,"

Bradford's face lights up with approval. "That is most heartening. A meeting between our leaders can only strengthen the peace you've begun."

Standish inclines his head. "Aye. It is wise to build understanding while the minds of both our peoples remain open."

I nod, satisfied. "We will return soon to meet with them again, as they suggested."

As we reach the Connor house, Henry and Danielle exchange a quiet nod and slip inside, taking the basket with them, and leaving Alyssa and me alone on the porch.

I know I shouldn't because someone might see us, but I take her hands in mine, and for a moment, the world narrows to her gorgeous green eyes, and the gentle press of her supple body against me. We hold each other in silence, the kind of quiet that says more than words ever could, until I finally step back.

"You should go inside," I murmur.

She nods, a smile touching her lips. "I'll see you tomorrow?" she asks.

"I'll be here at dawn if you'll have me."

"Oh, I'll have you," Alyssa says, her voice a perfect mix of sweetness and heat, sending a bolt of lightning straight through me.

I want to kiss her but force myself to walk away instead, watching her disappear inside the cottage.

The evening air is colder than I expect as I step inside my house, the door closing with a thud behind me, the memory of the day's encounters flooding my mind. I think not only of Alyssa and her incredible beauty, but my faith, my duty, my vows to my church creep in. My whole life, I've been warned against temptation, and yet, temptation appears so good, kind, selfless, loving, and ever so enchanting.

A knock shatters the quiet of the night. Who could be here after dark? Moving cautiously toward the door, I lift the latch. Moonlight spills across the threshold, and there stands Alyssa. Her face glows in the silver light, her features striking, framed by the night itself.

I hesitate, the air thick with warning. God above, I know I shouldn't invite her in, and yet every rational thought dissolves the moment I take her hand. I open the door fully, guiding her inside, careful, quiet, though my pulse is thunder in my ears.

She closes the door behind her, and we are alone. My hands find her waist. Her fingers lace through mine. Her lips meet mine, and it is not the brief, stolen kiss of yesterday. It is long, claiming, consuming. Every thought of right and wrong fades into the press of her body against mine. I am a lost wretch, and I never want to be found.

Finally, when my breath is ragged, and my knees threaten rebellion, I pull back slightly, resting my forehead against hers. "You must go," I whisper, the words tasting of bitter truth. "It's not right. We can't be caught together like this."

Her eyes shimmer. "I understand," she murmurs, though her fingers linger on my cheek. "I just couldn't stay away."

I feel the ache of restraint in my chest. "I was thinking of you when you knocked… I've not been able to stop thinking about you since we first met."

Alyssa presses her palm to my chest once more, then slips away, opening the door with a soft creak. It nearly breaks my heart to watch her go, and when she glances back, only once, her eyes shine like twin emeralds in the silver glow, before the darkness swallows her completely.

I stand rooted, listening to her footsteps fade into the night. Every prayer I know circles in my head, but none of them ease the longing clawing at my heart.

At last, I close the door and lean my forehead against the wood. The house is silent, but my soul is not. I whisper a prayer into the dark, knowing it will not be my last tonight.

WAMPANOAG

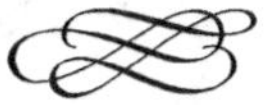

Alyssa

THE SUN RISES SLOWLY THIS MORNING AS OUR SMALL GROUP GATHERS outside the meetinghouse. I pull my shawl around my shoulders and glance toward Isaac and Henry, who are checking the fishing nets. Danielle and Samuel Tinker stand nearby, and my beautiful friend already has the boy laughing at something silly she's said before our day even truly begins. Young Samuel regains his composure partially, yet still shifts his weight from one foot to the other, restless with anticipation, pretending not to be excited but failing miserably.

Today, Samoset and Tisquantum are teaching us how to catch even more fish with nets.

Governor William Bradford finally arrives, buttoning his heavy coat. Captain Miles Standish follows close behind, his sword at his side, as always.

"Well," Bradford says, looking at our little group. "Let's see if your new friends will indeed show us the ways of this land."

"They will," Isaac assures him. "They keep their word."

We follow the shoreline, keeping our eyes open for any sign of the two men who have agreed to teach us. At last, we see them near the shallow edge of the bay. Samoset is tall and handsome, his strong facial features exuding masculinity. He motions toward the water with Tisquantum beside him, carrying a woven basket.

I learned of Tisquantum in my studies, and then later, I was able to teach my students about him. He's a Patuxet man, which is a band of Wampanoag. Wampanoag, means People of the First Light.

At this time, in the 1620s, there are about seventy villages that make up the Wampanoag and spread across the east coast of Massachusetts and even part of Rhode Island. It's interesting to think that I'm standing in my home state before states even existed, and yet the Wampanoag have been living here peacefully for over twelve thousand years.

Now that the Europeans have arrived, it will be only decades before these thousands become hundreds. A few years ago, Tisquantum was kidnapped and taken to Europe, where he learned English before finding his way home again. That's how he earns his place in the history books: as a translator for the newcomers who don't yet call themselves Pilgrims. Time and language, I've learned, are such fickle companions.

When we reach them, Isaac steps forward to make introductions. "Governor Bradford, Captain Standish, Samuel, this is Samoset and Tisquantum."

Bradford squints at Tisquantum, frowning. "It's a pleasure to meet the two of you. We've heard nothing but great things about you, Samoset and Squanto."

"Tisquantum!" we all respond in unison, voices ringing out across the water.

Bradford waves a hand dismissively. "Aye. Squanto. That's what I said," he repeats, though the exasperation in his tone only makes everyone grin.

Samuel Tinker's eyes go wide. "Tisquantum," he whispers, trying again, careful with each syllable. He looks up at Isaac for reassurance, and Isaac just nods with a smile.

Samoset chuckles, nodding to Bradford, while Tisquantum bows his head slightly.

Isaac puts a hand on my shoulder. "They are ready to show us," he says. "Shall we?"

"We'll teach you something new with the nets now," Samoset says.

We follow, the fog lifting to reveal water flashing silver in the morning light. Samoset and Tisquantum unwind the long nets and show us how to tie knots and anchor the nets with stones. Samuel crouches close, fascinated by every motion.

"You must leave space," Tisquantum explains, placing Samuel's hands where the knots go. "So the fish will swim in here, see? Now they can't escape."

Samuel grins. "Like a trap! But for fish!"

"Exactly so," Isaac says, kneeling beside him. "Think you can manage it?"

"I can do it faster than you," Samuel boasts, his fingers flying. He ties three knots in a row and looks up proudly. "See?"

Danielle laughs. "Show off."

Henry chuckles. "We'll let you catch dinner then, young Tinker."

Samoset demonstrates how to draw the net through the shallows, while Tisquantum gestures for us to try. The water is cold around my ankles.

Bradford, still on shore, watches with folded arms but an interested expression. "It seems," he says, half to himself, "our salvation may indeed lie with you men."

Tisquantum straightens, water glistening on his hands. "We share what we have and what we know," he says simply. "We can all work together."

I glance at Samuel, whose grin could outshine the sun, and hope stirs in my chest, fragile and bright, like the dawn breaking over Plymouth.

Isaac and I drift down shore from the others, nets in hand, the laughter of the group fading behind us. The water bends here, quiet and shaded by tall pines.

He looks dangerously handsome this morning with his hair tied back and the laces of his shirt undone just enough for me to see the outline of his chiseled chest. I daydream of running my fingers over those muscles and have to bite my lip when he glances over, his sleeves rolled to the elbow, water glinting off his strong forearms.

"You're quiet," he says, his voice low, almost teasing.

"Just… observing." I smile, thinking fast to change the subject before he can ask what I'm looking at. "This place feels so different when we are alone."

He steps closer. "You mean more peaceful?"

"Peaceful and safe." I tilt my head, meeting his eyes. "It's easy to forget where we are when everything is so serene and beautiful."

His gaze lingers on me for a long moment. "Miss Montgomery, there are a lot of things I forget when I'm near you." His words make me blush, and then he moves closer, barely an arm's length away. "I don't know what's happening," he says quietly. "You appeared here out of nowhere. You speak like no one I've ever met, and I truly can't stop thinking about you."

My heart thunders in my chest. I want to lean in, but I also know how dangerous this is for both of us. If we get caught kissing….

"We shouldn't be doing this," I whisper. "But I feel the same way about you, Isaac."

"Aye. We shouldn't. You're right," he agrees, though he doesn't move away. "Alas, I'd like to speak with you alone this evening. If you will permit it?"

I nod, trying not to smile too widely. "I'll tap on your back door when there's no one around, and everything's dark."

"Aye." His voice softens. "We'll speak then."

Before either of us can say more, Standish calls out to us from up the shore, and the moment shatters like ripples spreading across the water. Isaac clears his throat, stepping back. "We should return before they send the boy to fetch us."

"Samuel would find us in a heartbeat," I say, laughing.

When we wade back, the scene that greets us nearly makes me burst out laughing. Samuel Tinker has caught ten fish already, and he's shouting gleefully. Bradford and Standish, on the other hand, look positively grim beside their empty nets. Samoset and Tisquantum laugh openly, cheering Samuel on in his success.

"Look, Mistress Montgomery!" Samuel yells, holding up a wriggling trout almost as long as his forearm. "They keep swimming right to me!"

Bradford shakes his head in disbelief. "The boy has a charmed hand. What can we do?"

"A charmed hand or good teachers?" Henry says, nodding toward the Wampanoag men.

Tisquantum laughs, his eyes bright. "He listens well, that's all."

Samuel beams as he lowers his net again, water splashing high around his knees. Tisquantum and Samoset both smile, pleased with his enthusiasm.

When we're done for the day, Isaac steps forward and shakes their hands in thanks. "We owe you so much," he says sincerely. "You've shown us what we needed most."

"Now you know the sea," Samoset replies. "The sea feeds you and keeps you."

Henry bows slightly. "You've given us a gift we won't forget."

We walk them to the edge of the clearing, where they promise to return soon to teach us more of their ways. Samuel waves until they've disappeared into the trees.

By the time we return to the village, the sun is high, and our baskets are heavy with fish. The smell of salt and pine follows us, and Samuel can hardly walk straight for grinning. He keeps glancing into his basket like the fish might leap out and swim away.

"I caught twelve!" he crows, lifting the net so everyone can see. "Twelve huge fish!"

I laugh. "You're going to feed the whole colony, Samuel."

That's when the shouting starts. A cluster of townsfolk, at least a dozen men and women alike, are gathered near the common house. I recognize Priscilla Mullins in the front, her hands on her hips, and John Alden is beside her, looking equally cross.

"There they are!" Priscilla snaps, pointing straight at Danielle and me. "Now they've got the governor parading about with heathens!"

"Savages," someone mutters behind her. "They'll turn on us soon enough."

John Alden folds his arms. "It's one thing to wander off with the godless people by yourselves, but to drag our leaders along with you? Treacherous!"

"Insolence!" one of the women cries.

Samuel steps forward, clutching his basket. "They helped me catch these!" he says cheerfully. "They told us stories and showed me how to tie the knots in the nets right! They're not bad people!"

"That boy's been bewitched," another man growls. "Surely, you can't abide these evil, godless ways, Governor Bradford!"

William Bradford raises a hand. The murmuring stops as the crowd waits for him to agree with them, but he doesn't. He simply exhales, long and weary, and walks straight past the crowd toward his house, without a word or even a backward glance. The silence he leaves behind is deafening.

Captain Standish steps forward next, his eyes narrowing. "Governor Bradford's done talking sense into you lot," he says flatly. "If you don't like the company we keep, you can refuse the fish we bring back. See how long you last without supper."

A few of the louder villagers shrink back. Someone mutters. Another crosses her arms and huffs. Priscilla glares at me, color rising in her cheeks. "This is an outrage," she shrieks. "Mark my words, Mistress Montgomery and Mistress Whitman will bring ruin to this place!"

Isaac moves beside me, his voice calm. "No ruin will come from learning. Ruin comes only from fear."

Samuel smiles up at him. "And from being hungry!" he adds.

That earns a few reluctant chuckles from the bystanders.

Standish smirks. "The boy's got more sense than most of you. Now, if you'll excuse us, we've got fish to clean and no time for foolish talk."

He turns on his heel, and the rest of us follow, leaving the angry whispers behind. As we walk toward the fire pit, Danielle leans close and murmurs, "They can gossip all they want. We've got dinner."

I smile, glancing back at Samuel, whose laughter carries on the wind. For now, that feels like victory enough.

FOOLED AROUND AND FELL
IN LOVE

Alyssa

When night settles over Plymouth and the only sound is the rhythmic crash of the distant surf, I pull my cloak tighter and slip through the shadows between the cabins. The meetinghouse lantern has long since been snuffed out.

Isaac's home sits near the edge of the clearing, candlelight flickering faintly through the shuttered windows. I knock on the back door, three quick taps.

The latch lifts almost at once. Isaac's face appears in the narrow gap, his hair mussed, his expression softening when he sees me.

He opens the door, steps aside, and lets me in. A single candle burns on the table beside a loaf of coarse bread and two tin cups. The quiet feels heavy—and intimate.

"I half-expected you wouldn't come," he admits, closing the door behind me.

"After today? I needed to see you." I shrug out of my cloak. "I can't believe how they talked about us, as if helping someone learn to fish is sinful."

Isaac sighs and runs a hand through his hair. "They fear what they don't understand. They think safety comes from keeping the world small."

I step closer, my voice low. "And you don't?"

He looks at me for a long moment, his dark eyes twinkling in the dim light. "Not since you arrived."

The way he says it makes my pulse quicken. I look away, hoping I don't betray how flustered I feel. "The entire situation is ridiculous," I say quietly. "The accusations, the rumors, the whispers, and the fear. Danielle and I only want to help."

"I know." His voice is gentle now. "You truly see people, Alyssa. You don't place value on rank, titles, or even tribes. You see people for who they are and meet them where they are. That frightens some people because they can't do the same. They've been taught not to try."

"Isn't it foolish?" I ask. "How the very lessons Jesus taught—acceptance, understanding, patience and love—are the same ideals the people who believe they're following Him the closest are the most afraid of?"

"Aye. The Lord's true message is easily lost in terror of the unknown, in fright and confusion."

Something about his ability to see the world from a different perspective than his separatist peers endears me to him even more than his rippling muscles and his defined features.

I take another step closer until the hem of my skirt brushes against him. "And you?" I ask. "Do I frighten you, too?"

He smiles. "Constantly."

I laugh, but when he lifts his hand and brushes his fingers along my cheek, butterflies burst into sparks. Suddenly, I'm sure I want to be his.

"You shouldn't be here," he murmurs, his voice deep and gravelly, but he doesn't move away.

"I know, but it's worth it, no matter the risk," I say, pressing my hands to his chest and letting my fingertips slowly work the laces of his shirt loose.

He traces my cheek with his thumb, and when his lips find mine, I move my hands to his broad shoulders, sliding down the sculpted biceps that make me lose my mind even just imagining being held by him.

I press my body closer to his, my heart hammering, every nerve alive with anticipation. I've made up my mind that tonight will be our first night together, as long as he's willing, and the thought sends a thrill through me I can't contain. I'm acutely aware of his presence, of the warmth radiating from him. The pull between us is magnetic. I want to savor this moment just a little longer, knowing the night ahead will change everything.

When Isaac draws back, he studies me as though asking a question, and I answer by lifting my cap from my head and lying it on the table. Slowly, I undo the pins and let my blonde waves tumble down over my shoulders.

"May I touch your beautiful hair?" he asks.

I nod, my pulse quickening. He lifts his hands and threads his fingers through my locks, massaging my scalp with gentle pressure. His lips find mine again, and I feel myself slipping into a heady mix of comfort and desire, the warmth of his touch sending lightning bolts racing through me.

"I've never seen a young woman with her hair uncovered before," he murmurs.

I bite my lip, excitement flaring. "Then maybe you'd like to see more of me uncovered," I whisper, letting the hint of promise hang between us.

He swallows hard, taking his fingers out of my hair, and I feel the tension rise between us, a pull that's been building since we first met.

"Come with me," he says, lacing his fingers with mine as he leads me through the doorway to his bed.

"Before I show you how much I care for you," he says, "I want to tell you, I've never known a woman like you. I'm falling in love with you, Alyssa."

"I feel it, too." And this time, my lips claim his with a hunger I've never known before.

I pull back just long enough to look at him, my pulse racing, my lips still tingling from the kiss. I reach for the laces of my bodice, untying it, and letting the fabric loosen and reveal my curves. Moonlight falls across my shoulders and then across my bare breasts.

Isaac's eyes darken. He clenches his fingers at his sides. My hair tumbles around me. His eyes are fixed on me, and I feel the heat between us spike with every glance. In every subtle movement, I see just how much he wants me.

I let my dress fall to the floor, and Isaac traces the outline of my breasts so gently that I barely feel his fingertips dance across my skin. When I lean my head back and close my eyes, he becomes bolder, squeezing my breasts and kissing them. My moans invite him to explore, and he teases me with his tongue.

I grab the front of his shirt, tugging it off in a rush of desire. His chest, sculpted from hard work and discipline, responds beneath my hands, every muscle defined under my fingertips, driving a heat through me that leaves me trembling and drenched with need.

I trail my fingers down the lines of his shoulders and collarbone, reveling in the strength I can feel. He leans into me slightly, letting me explore, and I can sense the same anticipation mirrored in him, every movement pulling us closer.

Our hands moving quickly, the rest of my undergarments slip away, and he pulls his trousers off as we tumble onto the bed, our bodies pressing together.

"You're the most desirable woman I have ever laid eyes on," he whispers.

"Would you let me show you how good I can make you feel?" I ask, running my fingers up and down his cock.

"You mean there's more?" he asks, half-teasing.

"There's so much more." My voice is low and raspy with longing.

With a sigh and a moan, I mount him and watch his eyes fill with pleasure as I slide down onto him. He fills me up perfectly, and I ride him, building friction, ecstasy, and rhythm with each breath.

The tension between us finally shatters, leaving us both trembling and breathless, pressed tightly together. His warmth seeps into me, and I press even closer, as if holding him could make this feeling last forever.

When I lie down next to him, the world beyond the room slips away completely. My fingers glide along the line of his jaw, feeling his pulse beneath my cheek, and he lays his hand on my back, holding me close. The electricity that drew us together still lingers, coiling through us in waves.

We lie together, our heartbeats slowing, side by side, letting the night wrap around us, hoping that what's begun between us will only grow stronger from here.

GOD OF THUNDER

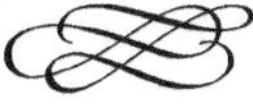

SUNLIGHT BLAZES IN THROUGH THE WINDOW, SHARP AND UNWELCOME, and I jerk awake, my heart hammering. My chest tightens when my gaze lands on Alyssa, still asleep beside me. Panic twists through me like a knife. It's dawn! People will see her leaving, and the village will talk. No, they'll accuse. They've already shouted witchcraft, and we've given them reason to shout sin and scandal. And worse… now fornication.

My stomach turns over. God forgive me.

I've sinned against her, against Him, and against everything I was raised to believe.

"Alyssa," I whisper, shaking her shoulder lightly. "We—we can't let anyone see you here."

She opens her eyes and smiles sleepily. "I know, Isaac," she murmurs. "It'll be fine. Don't worry. Don't let what others think of us make what we have any less special. We love each other."

I swallow hard, my love for her colliding with shame. "But we

105

have sinned," I confess. "Everything I've been taught all my life screams at me that we've done wrong, that I've led you into a snare."

Her hand finds mine, warm and grounding. "You haven't," she says, her voice firm. "We were together because we wanted to be. To show we care for each other. That's love, Isaac. Not sin."

I take a deep breath, allowing some of the guilt to ease away. "Then, we need a plan. I can't let anyone see you leaving. If the wrong eyes catch you, we could be banished—or worse."

Her brow furrows thoughtfully. "I could hide until dark tonight," she suggests quietly. "I could sit inside and hope no one notices my absence today."

I nod. "It's risky, but it might work."

Just then, there's a loud knock at the door. My blood freezes. No, no, no. Not now. Just our luck, it'll be Priscilla Mullins, or the governor, or Standish….

"Hide," I hiss, and Alyssa leaps up, wrapping a sheet around her unclothed body, and dives beneath the bed. I quickly make myself presentable, slide her clothing under the bed both to hide it and so that she can get clothed, and move to the door and crack it open a hair.

"Henry? Danielle?" I whisper, relief flooding me when I see their familiar faces. I pull them inside, closing the door quickly. "All is well. It's only our friends."

From beneath the bed, Alyssa peeks out, and I let out a breath. Her cheeks are pink, but the tension in her shoulders eases. I nod toward her. "You can come out. They won't tell a soul."

She steps out, straightening the dress she's manages to slide in even in such cramped circumstances. "Well, that solves that problem. It'll look like the four of us simply met here this morning. No sneaking, no scandal, no hiding required," Alyssa says.

Henry grins, nudging Danielle, who snickers beside him. "Kissing bandits," Henry teases, pointing at us. "Caught in the act, aren't they?" I'm relieved my friend has taken my side.

Danielle laughs. "You two Naughty Nellies!"

Henry laughs, and I clear my throat, my cheeks heating. Alyssa smirks, her shoulders lifting in amusement. The moment is light, teasing, and somehow safe. For now, we've skirted disaster.

"Very well, very well. I suggest we put aside all talk of kissing or banditry," I announce. "Samoset and Tisquantum showed us the valley beyond the ridge. There are massive herds of deer and elk there. If we go early, we could bring back enough to feed the village."

Alyssa nods, excitement lighting her eyes. "And we can pack food for the trail," she says, gathering a basket. "Bread, berries, dried meat."

Henry frowns thoughtfully. "A hunt, you say? That could be useful. Smoked meat may last longer than fish. We'll need tools, knives, baskets for the game, and someone strong to carry it all."

"I know just the boy," Alyssa says, her eyes sparkling. "Samuel Tinker. He's eager to learn and can help us carry what we kill."

Alyssa hurries out, returning a few minutes later with Samuel, wide-eyed and proud to be asked to come along.

We gather our weapons: matchlocks, bows, knives and then double-check our provisions. Henry carries his bow and quiver of arrows. Samuel tucks a small knife into his belt, practically vibrating with anticipation. Alyssa slings the picnic basket over her shoulder, and I shoulder my matchlock.

We walk for a long while before the valley opens before us, a vast meadow of tall grass and scattered trees.

Alyssa tugs at Danielle's sleeve, her eyes bright. "I saw ground cherries across the ridge," she says. "They're good for preserves and tinctures, and the seeds grow well in Plymouth. If we gather them, we could bring something useful back for the village."

Henry frowns, his hand resting on his bow. "That's quite a trek, and the path is tricky."

"We'll be careful," Danielle says. "They're rare, and I promise they're worth it."

Before we can protest further, the two women stride ahead, moving with purpose. Their voices carry faintly back to us, light and teasing.

Only as their figures shrink over the ridge do I notice the first gray threads pulling across the sky, darkening the sun's warmth. The wind shifts and gusts sharply through the trees entering the clearing.

I yell, "Come back!" but the wind carries my words away, scattering them across the slope. I can no longer see the women. I follow after them, as quick as I can go. Henry goes another way to try to find them.

Samuel struggles to keep pace, glancing at the tall trees and darkening sky. I push forward, calling the women's names, my heartbeat quickening. The storm arrives with a sudden downpour, wind lashing at the branches. Visibility drops, and the group is fully separated now, the women out of view somewhere ahead, Henry still within eyesight over to my left, and me lagging behind with Samuel, trying to keep an eye on the boy.

I curse under my breath, straining to see through the thick, black curtain of the storm. Alyssa and Danielle were just here, laughing and carrying the basket, but now their shapes are gone, swallowed by the darkness and the wind. Samuel is close behind me, shouting, trying to keep pace, but even his voice is nearly lost in the roar of thunder.

The valley that seemed so open and welcoming only moments ago has twisted into something unrecognizable. Every tree looks the same. Every ridge and hollow blurs before my eyes. The storm lashes at our shoulders, rain stinging like needles, and my boots slide on the slick undergrowth as I catch myself against a tree.

"Stay with me! Don't get lost!" I bark, but the words are almost useless. Henry's voice rises in reply, urging Samuel to hold fast, but the wind swallows everything. Samuel yelps as his foot slips on a mossy root, and I lunge forward to steady him, mud and water splashing up around us.

I skid down a small ridge, grabbing a tree trunk to keep from tumbling, and the valley tilts impossibly beneath me. The storm bends the world around us. I can't see the maidens, nor can I see the path we followed here. Henry calls out, his voice tight with worry, but I can't locate him either. Samuel clings to my sleeve, frightened, trying to follow, but the mud pulls at him.

The hunt has begun, yes, but not for deer. Alyssa and Danielle could be anywhere, and I have no idea which direction to run.

"Henry!" I shout, my voice cracking. Mud clings to my hands as I grab at tree roots, trying to keep from sliding further. Thunder booms, rattling me to the core, and lightning splits the sky, illuminating fleeting shadows. I think I see movement, perhaps a flash of Alyssa's cloak. Alas, it disappears in the next heartbeat, swallowed by the storm.

Samuel grips my arm, his teeth chattering. "I—I can't see them!" he cries.

"Neither can I!" I admit, my voice tight. "Keep close to me! Keep close to Henry!"

The valley is no longer a place to hunt deer. It is a labyrinth, a living trap, and the five of us are caught inside it. This storm appeared out of nowhere, and now, it threatens to destroy us.

Surely, this is not God's wrath for the sin Alyssa and I committed against Him? She said it was love, and God speaks highly of love. But we are not wed...

I lunge forward, mud sucking at my boots, calling their names again, but the storm steals the sound. Every flash of lightning reveals nothing but black shapes of trees and slick ridges. "We have to find them!" I shout, panic sharpening my words. "Alyssa! Danielle!"

Henry grabs my arm. "Isaac, we can't! The wind is too strong, the rain is too heavy, and we'll lose each other too if we go chasing blindly."

"They're out there! I couldn't keep track of them! I tried!" I grit my teeth, feeling guilt twist through me like ice. "I can't just wait while they wander in this!"

Samuel shivers beside me, gripping my sleeve. "I can't see! I don't want to get lost, too!"

I take a hard breath, forcing my shaking hands to unclench. "Samuel is a boy. I won't risk losing him in this. That's the only reason we stay."

Henry nods, his jaw tight, understanding without a word. The storm hammers the ridge, and the forest seems to shift beneath our feet.

I slide down a small incline, and something dark catches my eye. It's a hollow in the ridge, half-hidden by a boulder and brambles. "There!" I gasp, motioning. "It's a cave. We can wait it out in there!"

We scramble toward it, rain dripping down our backs. Inside, the hollow is narrow but dry, offering shelter from the storm. Samuel curls against the stone, his teeth chattering. Henry keeps watch at the entrance, his eyes sharp, his ears straining against the roar of the wind.

I sink to my knees, defeat rippling through me. I can't see them, can't hear them, and the guilt presses down hard. I failed to keep track of Alyssa. Yet, I remember her hand in mine, her voice telling me our love isn't sin. I would not undo what we shared last night, but what if it costs us everything? I love her, and that thought is a shred of warmth amid the cold, wild fury outside.

We huddle in the cave, listening to the storm batter the ridge, and all I can do is wait and pray. Yet, as I bow my head, a hollow fear grips me. I don't know if God still hears me after what I've done, but I trust in His mercy and pray for the strength to endure this storm, and those yet to come.

STORMS AND BEASTS

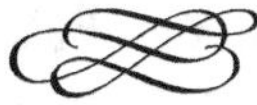

Alyssa

Rain lashes my face, sharp as needles. The wind howls so loud it swallows our voices whole. I clutch my skirt in one hand and reach for Danielle with the other, but I can barely see her through the torrent, her bonnet torn away, her hair plastered to her cheeks.

"Keep hold of me!" I shout, though the storm rips the words away. She grips my wrist as thunder crashes so close it shakes the ground.

We shouldn't have gone so far for the cherries. We are up on the tallest peak, and I can't even tell which direction the valley is now. Everything looks the same, gray and spinning. The rain blinds us, stings our eyes, soaks us to the bone. I stumble in the mud and nearly fall before Danielle hauls me up.

"There has to be shelter somewhere!" she cries.

Lightning splits the sky, illuminating the valley for one blinding heartbeat. I see a row of trees to the north, and the shimmer of a ledge of wet rocks. "There!" I point.

We fight our way toward it, slipping and sliding down the slope. I can barely breathe through the sheets of rain. The ground suddenly drops out from under me, and I tumble, landing hard on my knees.

"Alyssa!" Danielle scrambles down after me, clutching a low branch for balance.

"Over here!" I yell, motioning toward a hollow under the rocks, just enough of an overhang to block the rain. It's not much, but it's dry enough to breathe. We crawl under it, gasping for air.

For a while, we just sit there, shaking and dripping, our hearts pounding. The storm is deafening. Water rushes past in little rivers, carrying leaves and twigs downhill.

"This is insane," I mutter, wrapping my arms around my knees. "We're actually going to get struck by lightning in the seventeenth century."

She gives a breathless laugh. "That would be one way to make history."

Thunder rolls again, closer. I flinch, feeling it in my chest. "They'll be looking for us," I say. "Isaac and Henry–they'll come looking."

She nods but shifts her eyes toward the trees. "If they can even see through this."

Time drags on, frustratingly slowly as we wait, but eventually, the rain eases. The roar softens into a patter, and pale light filters through the clouds. Crawling from beneath the ledge, I push myself up, my legs trembling.

"Come on," I say. "We have to find them before they start worrying or before it starts pouring again."

We climb back up the incline. When we peer over, the valley looks completely different now, gray, dull, muted, misty, and empty. I hear no voices and see no movement. There's only the sound of dripping branches and the delicately noble fragrance of clean earth after a strong rain.

Danielle cups her hands around her mouth and calls out, "Henry! Isaac!"

Her voice echoes, unanswered.

A cold knot tightens in my stomach. "They were just over that rise," I whisper, scanning the hills, but the only thing staring back is fog.

"They'll find us," Danielle says softly, like she's trying to convince herself.

"Yeah," I say, forcing a shaky smile. "Or we'll find them."

The wind still howls through the trees, cold and wet, and droplets of rain fall on my face as Danielle and I push through the dripping ferns.

"Henry!" Danielle calls, her voice raw. "Isaac!"

No answer.

Danielle shakes her head, water streaming from her hair. "They wouldn't leave us."

I call again, louder. "Samuel! Isaac!"

The sound that answers isn't a voice. It's heavier, like something alive, shifting through wet brush.

Danielle goes rigid beside me. "What was that?"

Before I can answer, a low, guttural growl rolls through the trees. About fifty yards ahead, a dark shape moves between the trunks.

A young black bear, rain-slicked and furious, steps into view. Its eyes catch the slate light like coals, and when it huffs, steam rolls from its mouth.

"Oh, my God," I breathe.

Danielle clutches my hand. "What do we do?"

I can't think. All the rules I've ever read blur together. Don't run. Don't scream. Don't make eye contact. But the rules don't matter when it's right there, growling at us.

The bear snorts again, pacing. It's young, big enough to kill us but not old enough to be cautious.

"It's mad we were shouting," Danielle whispers.

I nod. "We must've scared him."

We start to back away, slow and trembling, but the bear steps forward, its muscles bunching beneath its fur.

"Don't move," I hiss, though I can't tell if I'm saying it to her or myself.

Another noise behind us has me whirling, afraid this bear has a friend. But before I take another breath, Isaac and Henry step out of the tree line, rushing to stand protectively between us and the bear.

"Stay still!" Henry whispers, his bow already raised.

The bear rushes toward us with a roar that shakes the ground. Henry draws and releases. The arrow streaks through the air and slams into the bear's eye. It bellows and rears up on hind legs, even more enraged. It's injured but definitely not dead.

Isaac lunges forward. "Get back!"

He drives his knife up underneath the bear's ribs. The death wail it bellows is horrible, wet and guttural. Then, the bear collapses straight onto him.

"Isaac!" My voice cracks as their bodies hit the ground with a sickening thud.

For a heartbeat, no one moves. My brain won't process what I'm seeing, only that the bear is still twitching, and Isaac is gone beneath it.

Danielle screams. I stumble forward, mud splashing up my legs.

Henry's already there, shoving against the bear's bulk. "Help me!"

We push together, shoulder to fur, grunting, slipping. It takes everything we have before the weight finally shifts enough for Isaac to drag himself free.

He's pale, gasping, his sleeve torn and blood soaking his shoulder. He tries to stand, and Henry catches him before he falls. "You're whole. You've escaped death."

Isaac nods weakly, though his breath rattles. "I had to finish the poor fellow."

Danielle cries softly beside me. I can't blame her. I want to cry, too, from the fear, the chaos, but mostly for the young bear, who lies still, its remaining eye glazed, the mud around it dark with blood. All I can think is how close we came to death and how easily it could've been one of us instead.

The rain softens to a mist by the time we start to calm. Samuel bursts through the trees, his face pale beneath his soaked hat. "Mercy above, what's happened here?"

Henry wipes his bowstring on his sleeve. "A bear charged the maidens, and we killed it."

The boy stares at the carcass, his jaw tight. "Killed it, did you? I miss all the sport!"

"You did well to stay put, boy," Isaac says. "You could've been hurt. We're all safe now, and that's all that matters."

Danielle crosses her arms. "I don't care if we never see a deer out here," she mutters. "I just want to go home, and it's going to take all of us to carry this fellow back. I think we should say a prayer of thanks for him."

"Carry him back?" Samuel asks.

"Of course," Danielle replies. "We can eat this big guy for a month. He can also be used for grease for dry skin, and look at his beautiful fur. What a marvelously warm blanket he'd make, don't you think?"

"Aye, Mistress Whitman," Samuel nods. "You know a lot about this part of the world. How do you know so much?"

Before Danielle can answer, I interrupt. "If we are going to eat bear, we better get him home and start cooking him before it gets too late."

Four of us grab a limb of the bear and begin carrying him toward the village while Samuel carries the basket.

"Lord God, over Heaven and Earth, thank you for this blessing," Henry says as we lug the beast through the woods.

Eventually, we have to take a short break and rest. Isaac and I stroll away from the group, until it's just the two of us.

"You saved my life," I say. "We could've died, Isaac. I was so scared."

He looks deep into my eyes. "I would do anything for you, Alyssa."

I press my lips to his quickly before Samuel can stumble upon us, and then we go back to the group.

We continue home, and soon the village roofs are just visible through the thinning trees.

Everyone marvels at the bear, and some of the villagers begin cleaning and preparing the beast for cooking. I turn to Isaac and ask if we can speak alone again, and he escorts me away from the group.

"Will you be all right? Should I bandage your wound?" I ask.

"Aye. It's barely a scratch, but if you wanted to check on it later…."

My pulse stirs. "Tonight?"

"After dark," he says quietly.

I nod once, my breath catching. "I'll be there."

For the rest of the evening, all I can think about is Isaac facing a bear for me. It feels almost surreal, like something from a storybook, and yet I can't stop thinking about how amazing both men were. The fear hasn't left me, and I know how close we came to disaster, but there Isaac stands, exhausted and yet unflinching.

I can't look away, caught between disbelief and how impossibly safe and protected he makes me feel.

THE VILLAGE IS QUIET AFTER DARK. ONLY THE WIND MOVES THROUGH the thatch, whispering over the rooftops. Lanterns glow faintly through shutter cracks, but most have been extinguished.

When I knock on Isaac's door, it's only once before it opens.

He's barefoot, his hair still damp from washing, the soft golden light catching on his cheekbones. He closes the door behind me.

"I've yearned for you all evening," he says.

I blush. "I couldn't stop thinking about you either."

He lifts a hand, hesitates, then reaches for my cap. His fingers run through my hair, brushing it back from my face. The warmth of his touch makes me shiver.

Isaac kisses me, gently at first, but when I lean into him, his restraint breaks. His hands find my waist, drawing me closer until I can feel his chest against mine.

And when he leads me toward the narrow bed, undressing us both as we go, the world outside seems to fall away.

As we tumble into bed, Isaac kisses my neck. He cups my breasts, teasing my nipples with his fingertips. I moan with pleasure and wrap my hand around his cock, which is already twitching with desire.

"Please take me," I whisper.

His eyes fill with lust as he moves between my legs. I groan at the immediate feeling of ecstasy and instinctively move my knees up to give him a deeper angle.

"Alyssa," he moans as he feels the shift in position, his pace quickening.

I lie back, his masculine body above me, and a hum of serenity and elation runs through me.

When he leans down and takes my breast into his mouth, a whimper of pleasure escapes me, and I watch him respond, the movement of his hips matching my reaction. Each stroke drives deeper, pressing against the places within that threaten to unravel me completely.

I start to climax, my body drawing him in as the pleasure peaks. He feels it, too, and we come together, hard and fast, lost in the intensity of the moment.

We lie together in the quiet of his small home, the candle flickering low, shadows dancing across the walls.

"I shouldn't have," Isaac murmurs, his voice heavy with guilt. "I shouldn't have let this happen again, not like this. It's just that you're so beautiful, and I love you so much, but Alyssa...."

"Isaac," I whisper. "You don't need to feel guilty. We have done nothing but show one another how much we care for and love each other."

He swallows, his jaw tight. "Alas, it could be very dangerous. If anyone knew, you could get in trouble, Alyssa."

"I know," I breathe. "I'm scared, too." I trace the curve of his arm. "But I can't pretend I don't want this. I can't pretend I don't want you."

He runs a hand through his hair. "You could get hurt. If anyone finds out what we did, they won't understand, and I can't bear the thought of anything happening to you because of me."

I close my eyes, leaning closer. "Then we'll be careful," I whisper. "I'll sneak back to the Connor house."

"Aye. And I'll worry about you the whole night, hoping you made it there safely, but not truly knowing."

"It's only a short walk. I'll be fine."

"Today, you were merely steps ahead of me when a storm and a beast both separated us. I thought I was going to lose you," he says, holding me even tighter.

I bury my face in his chest, trying not to cry. The comfort of his presence should ease everything, yet the gravity of what I carry feels heavier than ever. I wonder if marriage could solve some of the problems between us and give us a way to hold on to each other despite the danger around us.

In the most selfish part of me, I wish that instead of going into the dark, cold night back to the Connor house, I was going home to 2025. Yet, I love Isaac, and I want to stay with him, too.

How will I ever tell him that I'm from another time? Will it destroy everything we might have, and will I eventually have to leave him behind? I rest my head against his chest, near the scratch left by the bear, listening to his heartbeat, desperate for an answer I can't reach.

GUIDES

I SLIP QUIETLY THROUGH THE DARKNESS, THE CHILL OF THE NIGHT biting at my cheeks as I make my way back to the Connor house. My boots crunch softly against the frost-hardened ground, and I hug my cloak tighter around me. I can see the faint light spilling from the windows, and I know Danielle will be awake, watching over the children, waiting for me. I push the door open, careful not to make a sound, and step inside.

The warmth of the house hits me immediately, and I spot Danielle at the small hearth, her head bent, checking that the children are asleep. She looks up as I come in, her eyes narrowing slightly in concern. "Alyssa, what's the matter?" she asks quietly.

I sigh and drop onto the edge of the bed, staring at the floor. "I can't stop thinking about Isaac," I admit, my voice low. "Being with him is nearly impossible here, and yet, if we were living in the future, it would be so simple. It's like it's all being denied us."

Danielle tilts her head, her expression softening. "You mean because of all the religious laws?"

I nod, my fingers twisting in my lap. "Yes. I can't imagine marrying him and staying here, not really. Not when so much of this world is different, when everything is so dangerous, and I miss my family so much. I still miss home."

She moves closer and sits beside me. "Henry and I are struggling with the idea of being intimate as well. He can't get past his religious convictions, and I respect him. I don't mean to change him. Maybe you're right. Maybe it's time we stopped avoiding it. We can't stay stuck. We need a plan to get back or at least figure out if it's even possible. Last time we tried, we nearly drowned."

I swallow hard, my chest tight. "I've been thinking. The Wampanoag are wise, and they're so well connected with the natural world. Maybe they'll know how we could get back home. But, Danielle, I think we should tell Isaac and Henry where we are really from. They deserve to know the truth before we try to return home. Maybe that's why it didn't work the first time we tried. We never said goodbye."

She nods. "Agreed. I've had the same thoughts. We'll have to be careful. They definitely won't understand at first. We need to explain everything clearly."

I think through the next step. "After we tell them," I say slowly, "we need to speak with the healer, Kesuk, Obbatinewat's sister. If anyone knows if there's a way to get back to the future, it'll be her."

My friend squeezes my hand. "Then it's settled. Tomorrow, we tell the men, and then we go to her."

I lean back against the wall, letting the warmth of the fire seep into my bones. The plan feels fragile, like it could shatter with the smallest mistake, but at least it's something. At least it's a direction.

Danielle and I exchange a look of determination. We can face tomorrow together.

I put on a nightgown and slip into the bed beneath the warm blankets. The chill of the night finally fades, and with that, I drift into a restless sleep, knowing dawn will bring both hope and uncertainty.

THE MORNING SUN IS BRIGHT, BUT THE CHILL STILL CLINGS TO THE room. I watch the Connor children as they sit at the table, carefully eating the fried fish and berries Danielle and I have prepared. Their faces are brighter each day. Danielle passes another small piece to the youngest, and I take a deep breath, trying to ease the knot of anxiety tightening in my chest.

After breakfast, we settle the children with a game of tossing a beanbag back and forth, telling the oldest that he's in charge. Then, Danielle and I exchange a look. It's time.

We move toward the edge of the village, where the rhythmic sound of axes cutting wood echoes through the clearing. Henry and Isaac are there, swinging at a fallen tree for firewood, their muscles straining, with beads of sweat gleaming on their foreheads. I hesitate, glancing at Danielle. She nods, and we step forward.

"Gentlemen?" I call softly. Both men pause mid-swing, wiping their brows. Isaac narrows his eyes, alert, while Henry leans on his axe, curiosity blooming across his face.

"Good morrow, maidens," Isaac says cautiously. "What brings you here?"

Danielle smiles faintly. "We were hoping to speak with you for a few minutes," she says. "Somewhere private, if that's possible."

Isaac glances at Henry and then nods. "Aye. A short break wouldn't hurt," he says. "Tea inside my house?"

We follow them back to Isaac's cottage. He and I prepare the tea, and every time his hand brushes mine, I yearn to fall into his strong embrace and run away from the problems and pain I'm about to confess to him.

Once tea is served, I glance at Danielle. She gives me a small, tense nod, and I know we're both thinking the same thing.

This conversation can't be rushed, but it needs to be started.

I begin slowly, choosing my words carefully. "There's something difficult we need to explain," I say. "Something about who we are and where we really came from."

Isaac frowns. "You've told us where you're from. Bristol, England."

Danielle takes over. "That wasn't true. I made that up in order to protect us from being called liars, or worse, witches."

"A lot of good that did us," I mutter.

"What do you mean, Danielle?" Henry asks.

"Well, we aren't from Bristol. We are from here. We were born and raised right here in Plymouth."

"Surely you mean Plymouth, England?" Isaac asks.

"No. We were born right here in Plymouth, Massachusetts. Only we were born in the year 2003, and it was 2025 when we got into an accident and ended up here."

Isaac looks at me with disbelief spreading across his face. Henry's jaw drops. Both men exchange an incredulous look.

Henry finally asks. "We're meant to believe you've... traveled through time?"

I nod. "We know it's hard to accept, but there are things we can describe and events, places, things from the future that no one here could possibly know."

Isaac runs a hand through his hair. "I don't know," he mutters. "After the storm, the bear, Priscilla Mullins and her friends calling you witches, and the pressures of our religious laws, perhaps your minds are overwhelmed. I'm sorry, but I can't believe you."

Henry shakes his head, still skeptical. "Either you lied about who you are and where you came from when we first met you, or you're lying now, and I can't abide liars. We've heard enough for one day."

The betrayal in their voices is sharp and cold, a knife to the gut. I take a deep breath, keeping my frustration in check.

"We should get back to the children," Danielle says smoothly, standing.

Isaac and Henry nod, returning to their axes when we leave the cabin. I exchange a look with Danielle, and we know there's no turning back from what we're about to do.

Instead of returning to the children, we step away from the clearing, and without another word, we veer into the woods, leaving the village behind, our plan unspoken but alive in our minds.

The forest is dense as Danielle and I push through brambles and low-hanging branches. Each rustle of the underbrush makes me jump. Each birdcall seems sharper than it should. My thoughts keep drifting to Isaac and Henry, still back in Plymouth, chopping wood and unconvinced by our story.

"I hope we bump into Samoset soon," I whisper, trying to keep my voice low.

Danielle pushes a low branch out of her way. "He always seems to be fishing. We just need to make it to the bay."

Finally, through a narrow break in the trees, I see movement ahead. Samoset strides easily over the uneven ground, familiar and reassuring. Beside him, a tall, broad-shouldered man steps from the shadows.

"Alyssa! Danielle Big-Fan! How are you today?" Samoset asks.

"We are better now that we found you," Danielle replies.

"This is my friend Hobbamock," Samoset says, introducing him with a small bow. "He is a warrior and guide." Turning to Hobbamock, he continues, "These maidens are Alyssa and Danielle Big-Fan. They are friends of ours from the shore."

Hobbamock inclines his head slightly, a silent greeting that carries respect and acknowledgment.

Danielle and I respond in kind, and then I turn to Samoset. "We were hoping you could help us find Kesuk, the healer. We have questions for her."

Samoset agrees to take us to Kesuk, and we follow the men, slowly winding through the forest. The path twists and turns over roots and fallen branches, past a small stream glinting in the morning sun. My legs are sore, my lungs burn from the effort, but each step carries a mix of optimism and apprehension.

At last, the forest opens onto a wide clearing, bustling with life. Dozens of Wampanoag men, women, and children move among small, conical homes woven from saplings and thatch, their surfaces painted with streaks of ochre, red, and white. Some tend fires, the smoke curling upward, while others carry baskets of berries or bundles of corn. Children chase one another barefoot through the soft grass. Men sharpen spears and trim arrow shafts, their long hair pulled back with leather, and a few wear decorative beads that glint with bright colors. Women squat by small clay pots, grinding corn or kneading dough, their braids swinging over shoulders.

Samoset and Hobbamock guide us across the clearing, past the families at work, until we reach a smaller, more secluded part of the village.

There, seated on a woven mat, is the healer we came to find. Her silver-streaked hair is braided over one shoulder, the dark strands gleaming beneath the gray. She wears layered robes of soft hide and cloth in deep earth tones, the subtle folds and stitching suggesting careful craftsmanship. Beside her stands a young maiden with striking dark eyes and a beautiful bone structure. She could've been a model in our time. Her garments are carefully fitted deer hide and woven fabrics, warm browns with subtle reds and whites woven into the seams.

Samoset inclines his head slightly toward the girl and says softly, "Tekoa will speak for her grandmother."

Hobbamock gives a slow, respectful nod as he and Samoset leave us to speak with Kesuk.

The bustle of the clearing fades in our awareness as we step closer, the healer's presence commanding our attention, the granddaughter at her side ready to bridge the worlds that separate us.

I take a deep breath. "We have something to tell your grandmother that will be unbelievable at first, but we desperately need her to believe us because we need her help." The girl nods, and I blurt out our secret before I lose my nerve. "We are from another time—from the future," I begin. "We need to return there, but we don't know how. Maybe she can help us."

Tekoa repeats my words in their language, and Kesuk listens intently. Then, she translates her grandmother's response: "The waters will open for one of you when the moment comes. Until then, guard the love that binds you, for it will light your way through the darkness. Remember the unborn life will be tied to the choices you make, a beacon across the years."

I glance at Danielle, my stomach twisting. "What? One of us? How will we know which one?"

"Unborn life? Which one of us will return? Ask her, please?" Danielle begs Tekoa.

"The healer has spoken," Tekoa says, and we fall silent, understanding that their custom allows no questions after the healer has given an answer.

We bow, gratitude and frustration tangled together. At least, Kesuk seemed to believe us. As Samoset and Hobbamock guide us back through the forest, the healer's words are heavy on my heart. The path is long, each step through the trees echoing the uncertainty we carry.

One of us will return. I don't understand how it will be decided, or who it will be, and I can't bear the thought of being separated from Danielle.

"The unborn life must be whichever one of us gets to go back home," I say.

"You mean because technically we haven't been born yet?"

"Don't you think?" I ask.

Danielle just shrugs. We're both more confused than ever, and I feel like I need a break from the whole situation and everyone involved.

Yet, somehow, I still ache for Isaac, wishing he would believe me and that he could see that I'm telling the truth. At the same time, I long to be back in 2025, to see my family, to be somewhere familiar, somewhere safe.

The choices before me feel impossible, the future uncertain, and all I can do is keep moving forward, hoping for a sign, a path, anything that might guide me home.

AMERICA, FOOTBALL, AND PUMPKIN PIE

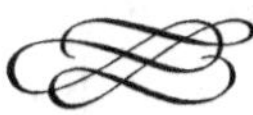

ISAAC

Isaac

Henry and I walk the worn path toward the meetinghouse. The bell hasn't yet rung, but we can already see men and women gathering, their faces solemn beneath wide-brimmed hats and linen caps. The Sabbath demands reverence, though my mind is far from peaceful.

Henry kicks a stray stone and glances my way. "I still can't make sense of what they told us," he says quietly. "That foolish story about being from another time. What could possess them to say such a thing?"

I let out a dry laugh. "Aye, 'tis the maddest thing I've ever heard. No one can travel through time, Henry. God alone ordains the days of men."

He nods but frowns. "It's madness, but it would explain a great deal, wouldn't it? The words they use, the information they know. Alyssa knows about hunting and tracking like I've never seen in a woman, and Danielle once said she wished she had 'batteries.' I still don't know what that means."

I can't help but smile at that, though it fades quickly. "It would explain much about them both," I admit. "Their confidence, their way of speaking. They're certainly women who fear no man's judgment. Alyssa looks every man in the eye. No Puritan woman does that."

Henry gives a low chuckle. "Aye, Danielle, too. She argues as though she were born to do it. Sometimes I think she means to undo me with her tongue alone."

We both laugh softly, but the weight of what he said settles in my chest. If it were true, if they truly came from some other time, then how could I ever keep Alyssa? The thought is foolish. She's flesh and blood, standing in the same sunlight as I am.

As we near the meetinghouse, the smell of damp timber and wool fills the air. Women and children go in first, settling on one side, while the men take the benches opposite. The room is plain with bare beams overhead, no ornament save for the pulpit. Henry and I remove our hats and nod to those we pass.

Alyssa sits stoically, her hands folded and her hair tucked away beneath her cap, though a few pale strands escape. My heart lifts at the sight of her, as it always does.

When our eyes meet, I nod slightly, offering her a smile. Henry does the same toward Danielle, but neither woman returns the greeting.

They turn their heads at once, as though they've not seen us at all. Alyssa looks down at her lap, her face unreadable.

Henry's brow furrows. "Did they—?"

"Aye," I murmur, my throat tight. "They saw us."

I try to console myself, to remember that we are in God's house, but a strange ache swells inside me. Alyssa has been distant these past few days, ever since that talk of time and worlds beyond ours. I thought it was nonsense. Yet, now she looks at me as though I'm the fool.

Elder Brewster's voice rises, calling us to prayer. We bow our heads, though my thoughts race. The sermon stretches long, with words about growing in patience, faith, and endurance, but I hear little of it. Every verse feels heavy, like a rebuke aimed straight at my heart.

When it's done, the congregation stands. William Bradford steps forward, his tone measured but warm. "Friends," he says, "the Wampanoag people have helped us survive these last few weeks. We owe much to Squanto and Samoset, who have shown us friendship and aid in this wilderness. I would have a feast of gratitude. I ask Master Owens, Master Lewis, Mistress Montgomery, and Mistress Whitman to find these new friends and extend our invitation to join us in a meal of camaraderie."

All eyes turn toward us. My chest swells with pride. It's an honor to be chosen, and a joy, too, that I'll see Alyssa beyond these walls.

Henry answers for us all. "We would be glad to, Governor."

I nod in agreement. Alyssa glances up then, just for a moment, but then she turns away.

When the meeting is finally done, the Sabbath half spent, I walk out into the sunlight with a heart as heavy as stone. Pride battles sorrow within me. I've been given a noble task, and in the company of the woman I love, but for the first time since meeting her, she feels a world away.

The afternoon light melts across the clearing as Henry and I make our way toward the Connor residence. The village has settled into its quiet rhythm again. Women hang linens, men tend fires, and children chase one another between the cabins. Yet, I cannot shake the nagging pain in my heart.

When Henry knocks, Danielle answers almost immediately, her eyes cautious but kind. She steps aside to let us in, and the scent of stew greets us. Alyssa stands at the hearth, spoon in hand, stirring a pot while the Connor children sit waiting.

"Mistress Montgomery," I say, trying to sound lighter than I feel. "We've come to speak of tomorrow's feast."

Alyssa looks up but doesn't quite look me in the eye.

Henry glances at Danielle. "Would you please take a stroll with me before your evening meal, Mistress Whitman?"

Danielle agrees, though she looks a bit wary, wrapping her shawl about her shoulders, and the two slip out the door.

I move to help Alyssa ladle food into wooden bowls, and together we serve the children. They chatter softly between bites, unaware of the tension pressing in around us.

"I apologize," I say finally. The words come out rougher than I mean them to.

She shakes her head, not looking at me. "You don't need to apologize. You were only being honest."

But there's something behind her voice, an ache, a distance that haunts me. I wish I understood her. I wish I could take away whatever burden she's carrying, but I still can't believe the story she told. It's too far beyond reason.

"Perhaps," I offer gently, "you just need some rest. The storm, the bear—it's been a long few days."

Her head snaps up then, her eyes flashing. "Please go, Isaac."

I open my mouth, but she turns away. The finality in her tone leaves no room for argument. I step outside, the door closing softly behind me.

The path home feels longer than ever. The air is cool, the sky deepening toward dusk. For the first time in my life, I feel truly hollow, like someone precious has slipped from my grasp, and I don't know if I'll ever reach her again.

THE NEXT DAWN IS CLEAR AND BRIGHT. HENRY, ALYSSA, DANIELLE, AND I walk the narrow trail west of the settlement, our breath rising in faint clouds. The forest hums softly with life: birds flying overhead, the rustle of squirrels, the distant crash of the sea. It should be a pleasant morning, yet there's a strange stillness between us.

Danielle walks beside Henry, their heads bent close as they speak in low tones. Whatever distance lay between them yesterday seems gone now. She laughs once, and Henry's grin flashes in return. I should be glad for him, but envy prickles all the same.

Alyssa walks ahead of me. She hasn't spoken a word to me since yesterday. I try to think of something, anything, to say, but every phrase dies before it reaches my tongue.

Danielle suddenly glances over her shoulder. "Alyssa, what's your favorite Thanksgiving food?"

Alyssa's lips curve faintly. "Oh, that's easy—mashed potatoes and gravy, with real gravy, not the kind that comes from a packet."

Danielle laughs. "You always say that! Mine's pumpkin pie. No, stuffing. Wait, maybe cranberry sauce."

Henry frowns. "Stuffing? Cranberry sauce? And what, pray tell, is Thanksgiving?"

I watch Henry's face, and I can't help but notice the way he lingers on Alyssa and Danielle, his expression serious, almost as if he's starting to believe them.

The women exchange a look, one of those wordless glances they share, like they're deciding how much truth to tell. Then Danielle smiles. "It's a celebration we have back home, in our time."

"What are you celebrating?" Henry asks.

"Well, today, actually," Danielle replies. "We're celebrating the very same events this feast is for."

"Today is the first Thanksgiving. I still can't believe we are here for it," Alyssa adds, a dreamy, far-away look in her eyes.

"It's a day when families gather to eat and give thanks for what they have," Danielle continues, "to celebrate the relationship between the first Plymouth settlers and the Wampanoag people."

Henry's steps falter. "You mean four hundred years from now, they will still be honoring this very day?"

Alyssa nods. "Centuries from now, people will not only remember it, but it's a very important day each year. They'll have parades with giant balloons floating down the streets, and football games on big glowing screens. Everyone eats turkey, potatoes, and pie until they can't move."

"Balloons? Glowing screens?" Henry asks.

"Football?" I add, unable to hold back my curiosity any longer.

Danielle giggles. "Football is a game people play in our time. It's one of America's favorite pastimes."

"America? Is that what they'll call the New World?" I ask.

For the first time in days, Alyssa truly looks at me. "America is what they'll call this country, but it's not new. The Wampanoag and millions of other people already live here. But yes, that's what they'll call this place one day. Danielle and I were born here, so we call ourselves Americans."

In that instant, seeing her standing there, speaking so confidently of worlds and wonders I can't begin to fathom, I feel the last of my disbelief slip away.

THANKSGIVING

Isaac

THE EVENING AIR HANGS CRISP, BUT THE CLEARING IS BRIGHT WITH firelight. Smoke from small hearths curls lazily toward the darkening sky, glowing amber in the last rays of the sun. Settlers and Wampanoag alike move among one another, arranging tables, benches, and baskets.

I walk beside Alyssa, her hand brushing mine as we thread between the gathered groups. Danielle and Henry trail just behind, speaking flirtatiously, though quietly enough I cannot make out their words.

Once we are all seated at long tables with mismatched benches, chairs, and stumps around a fire, Governor Bradford rises from his seat near the center of the main table. He scans the assembly, landing briefly on each familiar face.

"Friends," he begins, his voice strong but warm, "we gather this evening to give thanks to the Almighty for our survival, for the first harvest, and for the guidance of those who have shown us the way in this new land." He pauses, nodding toward Tisquantum and Samoset.

"And we honor those whose courage and wisdom have made this day possible."

Tisquantum stands, his voice clear and measured. "We give thanks for life, for the harvest, and for the guidance of friends. We honor those who have endured and those who have shown courage."

I glance at Alyssa, who leans toward me slightly, her green eyes shining in the firelight. "This is even better than I imagined," she whispers.

I nod, squeezing her hand gently.

Then Massasoit Obbatinewat speaks, his spirited voice and melodic language commanding attention. He speaks in Wampanoag, and Samoset translates. "We honor the courage of those who traveled far to survive and the hearts that welcomed them. We honor the harvest, and we honor the land that sustains us all. Let this day mark peace between our peoples and gratitude for what is given."

Bradford steps forward again, lifting a small loaf of bread. "We share this bread as a symbol of our unity. Let all who partake remember the kindness and courage that have brought us here. Let us honor the lives lost and the lives that remain, together."

I reach for a piece, glancing at Alyssa. A smile spreads across her face. Danielle leans toward Henry, her shoulder brushing his, and I see the way he relaxes, a small laugh escaping him at something she says. Around us, the whole village listens carefully.

Alyssa leans slightly against me, her breath warm against my shoulder. "It feels peaceful here today," she murmurs.

I nod. "It's the closest thing to true peace and unity I've ever felt." I glance at the fires flickering in the dimming light and imagine these flames in a fireplace far in the future, in a house I cannot fathom, and try to imagine others celebrating this day four hundred years from now. I cannot comprehend it.

As the speeches come to a close, they're replaced by laughter, chatter, nods of understanding, and the creak of benches and mats. Even without a shared language, the Wampanoag communicate well with us in gestures, glances, and expressions, bridging the gulf of difference with patience and respect.

Samoset leans toward me, his voice low enough that only I can hear. "My people understand the gift of this day, even if our words don't match yours."

I smile at him, wishing there were a way for him to know what Alyssa has told me, but I cannot pretend to explain it.

Bradford claps his hands. "Let us begin the meal." Baskets and bowls are passed, plates set down, and spoons lifted.

As everyone enjoys the feast, Alyssa leans in to tell me something, her eyes bright with childlike enthusiasm. She nods across the clearing to a young girl I don't recognize. "That's Tekoa. She's Kesuk's granddaughter. She speaks English, too. She learned it from Samoset."

Samuel Tinker sits near Tekoa. They carry themselves with a mixture of shyness and curiosity. I see him offer to help with a basket, and she smiles briefly, accepting. Soon, they are seated side by side on a log, leaning slightly toward one another, laughing over some shared jesting. I can see the spark of mutual interest forming, gentle and proper.

A warmth settles over me. I glance at Alyssa. She notices, too, and we share a brief grin. The sense of connection, of young hearts finding companionship, adds to the glee of the evening.

A hush ripples through the gathering. For a moment, no one breathes. Beside me, Alyssa stills, eyes wide, her hand pressed lightly to her mouth. Then her expression softens—surprise giving way to a quiet, radiant smile.

"It is our wish," Henry continues, "that the union be solemnized before winter's end, as God allows."

Elder Brewster nods his approval. "Then may the Lord bless and keep you both."

Warm murmurs spread through the tables—soft laughter, a few words of blessing. Danielle lowers her head, cheeks flushed, and Henry's hand finds hers.

Alyssa exhales, a laugh trembling in her voice. "She didn't say a word," she whispers, eyes shining.

I smile back. "Aye, but look at her. She's never been happier."

The sound of voices swells again, fires crackle, and the scent of smoke and roasted fowl drifts through the cool evening air. For a moment, everything feels lighter—brighter—than it has in weeks.

I smile at Alyssa, feeling merriment for our friends. Even across cultures and languages, the happiness is shared, palpable in the firelight and the warmth of the assembled people, and everyone seems even more delighted than before.

After a moment, Governor Bradford lifts a hand to still the crowd. Captain Standish follows, a quiet, approving nod accompanying his smile. Bradford speaks, and Samoset translates for the Wampanoag: blessings, prayers, and words of encouragement for the newly promised couple. Captain Standish places a hand lightly on Henry's shoulder, a gesture of guidance and approval.

Alyssa's face glows in the firelight, and I feel a rare stillness settle over me. She smiles, and I return it, letting myself savor the warmth, the laughter, and the simple joy of being here beside her. Whatever the future holds, tonight, this shared meal, these moments of peace, are comforting.

As the meal ends and the last of the Wampanoag and settlers rise from the benches, Alyssa and I move quietly among the tables, helping gather empty bowls and baskets. I feel a warmth settle in my chest, not just from the marriage announcement, but from the connections I've witnessed and the bonds formed this evening between so many.

When the clearing grows quieter, I approach Alyssa. "Would you permit me to walk you back?" I ask.

She nods wordlessly, her pretty eyes sparkling up at me. The path to the Connor house is hushed beneath the stars. The nearby forest is silent except for the occasional call of an owl.

My words tumble out in a rush. "Alyssa, I need to tell you that I was wrong to doubt you before. I should have believed you. You really are remarkable, and the things you know, the way you move through this world, in ways I can't even fathom... I love you for it. I love you for everything you are."

"Do you believe me now?"

"Of course I do," I confirm. "I should've believed you all along."

"Do you understand why we told you we were from Bristol and that we were world travelers rather than time travelers?"

"Aye. I'm sure that was a difficult position to be in."

"I'm so sorry we were misleading," she adds. "I promise never to be even the slightest bit dishonest with you ever again. I hope you can find it in your heart to forgive me."

"I forgive you," I tell her as we step apart. "You've carried so much, and you've guided me, too. I don't deserve you, Alyssa, but I'll spend every day trying to be worthy of you."

She smiles, radiant in the moonlight, the kind of gesture that quiets every fear and every lingering doubt. "You already are," she says simply.

I walk her to the door of the Connor house, waiting at the threshold, reluctant to let the evening end. She waves softly, and I turn back toward the path home, my chest lighter than it's been all day. The moon casts silver across the fields, and the cool night air brushes my face, but inside, I carry the glow of the evening, the laughter, the blessings, the promises, and the love I now know is real.

LOVE IS ENOUGH

THE EMBERS FROM LAST NIGHT'S FIRE STILL SMOLDER IN THE HEARTH, sending ribbons of smoke through the Connors' small house. The children are still asleep in the bedroom, bundled under patched blankets. Danielle's already up, tidying the table with a soft hum, and I can't stop smiling at her.

She's been glowing since the announcement. There's a lightness in her I haven't seen in, well, maybe ever.

"I still can't believe it," I whisper, grinning. "You're actually going to be a bride." I don't chide her for not telling me in advance, though I wish she would have.

She laughs under her breath, her cheeks pink. "It feels like I'm still dreaming. He was so nervous, Alyssa. His hands were shaking."

"His voice, too," I tease. "But it was perfect."

We both fall quiet, the memory of the feast still vivid–Henry making his announcement, the Wampanoag watching curiously as joy filled the clearing. It had felt like something sacred, a promise made under a new sky.

"I'm happy for you," I say softly. "Really happy. But aren't you scared?"

Danielle stops wiping the table. "Of what?"

"Of everything," I admit. "This century: the freezing temperatures, people getting sick, how there's never enough to eat here. Winter's coming fast. If we stay…."

I trail off, glancing toward the window where frost rims the edges of the oiled paper covering it where glass would be in my time.

She folds her hands, her expression turning thoughtful. "I've thought about it every day, and I'd rather face a harsh world with Henry than a comfortable one without him."

Her words hit me harder than I expect. I want to believe that love is enough to fight off hunger and cold, but part of me still aches for what we left behind: hot showers, soft beds, a stocked refrigerator, and doctors and medicine for illnesses and injuries.

"Sometimes I miss the noise," I whisper, "the lights, knowing what's going to happen tomorrow. Back home, everything made sense."

Danielle smiles. "And yet, here you are, still thinking about Isaac."

"I am… and yet, I don't know what I'm going to do. I don't want to leave any of you, but I'm not as certain as you about my place here."

"Do you love him?"

I nod. "I do. I just wish loving him didn't mean giving up everything else."

She reaches out and squeezes my hand.

"All right," I say, smiling. "If you're really getting married in 1621, we've got some serious planning to do."

Danielle laughs, and suddenly the room feels warm again. The future may be uncertain, but love feels like the one thing worth celebrating.

"Tomorrow," she says, gripping my hands. "Right after the church service."

I can't help but laugh. Her enthusiasm is contagious. "Then we'll have to move fast. What do you want it to look like?"

"Simple," she says, but her smile turns mischievous. "Simple and beautiful. Flowers if we can find them, pine boughs, maybe holly, and I want a veil with my hair down."

"A veil? Are you sure they'd allow that?"

"I don't care what's allowed," she says without hesitation, her voice tinged with determination. "It's my wedding. I only get one."

I grin. "Then we'll make it happen. You'll need something for your hair, something for the tables, and lots of delicious food. I think Kesuk or Tekoa might know how to weave grass cords that would look beautiful for tying bouquets."

Danielle nods, already in motion. "Let's go find Henry and Isaac and delegate some of the to-do list."

When we find the men, they're stacking wood behind the meetinghouse for Sunday's service. Danielle waves. "We need to get ready for tomorrow," she says excitedly. "Henry, we still have so much to prepare."

Henry laughs, brushing a hand through his hair. "I know, I know. The service is early, and then the celebration. There's still so much to gather."

Danielle nods toward us. "Alyssa, Isaac, could you please help by inviting our Wampanoag friends? We want them all to come. They've been so kind and generous to us. They should be part of this."

We agree to be the messengers, and I fall into step beside Isaac as we make our way through the woods toward the Wampanoag camp. The chill bites at my cheeks, and the smell of damp pine needles and frost on the ground reminds me, strangely, of the autumn walks on my grandfather's land not far from here.

A pang of longing twists in my chest, and I realize just how homesick I am. I wish I could somehow gather Danielle, Henry, and Isaac and bring them all back with me to the future, just for a little while, so I wouldn't have to feel this ache of missing everything I've ever known. My facial expression must betray me because Isaac glances at me with a look of concern.

"Is something amiss?" he asks.

I force a smile, unsure how to explain the ache. "I don't know how much longer I can stay here. I'm much more homesick than I thought I would be."

"You miss your family?"

I nod. "My parents, my brother James, and my sister Chloe. I think about them every day, and now, if I return home, I'll have to leave Danielle to start a new life with Henry. She and I have been together since we were five. I've never been without her. I don't know how I'll manage returning to 2025 without her… that is… if I figure out how."

"You have my support and my love, no matter what you decide to do," he says. "I will always love you."

I look up at him, tears brimming my eyes. "Thank you, Isaac, but that makes it even more difficult."

"How do you mean?"

"Well, couldn't you be more of a jerk? Why do you have to be so perfect?"

"Jerk?"

"It's a mean person, a bad guy, someone who jerks your heart around. And you—you are the most patient, understanding, and kind man I've ever known."

He leans closer, and when his lips meet mine, it's slow and urgent at the same time, a promise without words. I let myself melt into it, the tension, the fear, the longing of the past days pressing against me, and somehow, in that one kiss, it all softens me.

Then he exhales, resting his forehead against mine. "As much as I'd rather stay right here," he murmurs, his voice low and rough, "we should keep moving and finish our errand."

I let out a shaky breath and nod, though part of me wants to ignore him and stay hidden with him in the trees. Still, I take his hand, and together we start down the path again.

We reach the clearing where our Wampanoag friends have been working. Tekoa is there, her braids swinging as she lifts a basket. Her grandmother Kesuk is nearby, checking supplies for the coming winter.

"I'm glad to see you," I say, my breath forming small clouds in the crisp air. "We wanted to invite you to a wedding tomorrow, after the church service. Danielle and Henry are getting married."

Tekoa's eyes fill with joy, and a shy smile curls her lips. "I will tell everyone," she says enthusiastically.

When she translates for her grandmother, the wise healer nods and responds to her granddaughter.

"My grandmother says she's sure everyone will come. We will bring food and music with us. Kiehtan will bless your friends."

A warmth spreads through me at their acceptance. We thank Tekoa and Kesuk for passing along our invitation and bid them farewell until tomorrow.

We walk back to the village, ready to dive into wedding preparations. Isaac and I join Henry and Danielle, sorting supplies and making plans. Surrounded by friends and laughter, the work feels good, and for now, the day ends on a quiet, contented note.

THE NEXT DAY'S CHURCH SERVICE HAS ENDED, AND I FOLLOW DANIELLE to Governor Bradford's house and into the small room beside the main living quarters. She stands in front of me, smoothing the veil we made together, her hands trembling slightly with excitement. I watch her, knowing this is her big moment.

When we step into the main room, Danielle's eyes sparkle with nervous excitement. She straightens, taking a deep breath, and Henry waits across the space, his gaze fixed on her. For a moment, nothing else exists, just Danielle, radiant and stunning, and Henry, full of awe and love. Many people are gathered inside, with the crowd spilling out into the yard since we've invited our Indigenous friends.

A few people whisper about Danielle's hair, but we ignore them. The veil covers it, even if it is down and not hidden beneath a cap.

The ceremony is simple, yet every word carries a lifetime of longing. Danielle's hands tremble slightly as she reaches for Henry's, not from fear, but from the weight of this moment: this is the first time she's ever truly belonged somewhere and the first time she's been able to imagine a family of her own.

Her eyes glisten as she meets his, and I see the quiet surrender in her expression, the trust and love that has been waiting for this day her entire life. Henry's gaze never wavers as if he's holding not just her hands, but the fragile hope she's carried alone for so long.

When Governor Bradford pronounces them husband and wife, the congregation erupts in smiles and cheers. Danielle's face shines with happiness as Henry lifts her hand to his lips.

After the ceremony, we move to the feast clearing, now bustling with tables laden with food. Settlers and Wampanoag alike mingle, bringing dishes of roasted game, corn breads, fruit preserves, and nuts from the forest. Smoke rises from bonfires, mingling with laughter and chatter. Danielle greets the guests. Henry beams at her, and she leans toward him, whispering something that makes him chuckle. I can't help but grin, watching their love in motion.

Samuel and Tekoa gravitate toward each other during the meal, quietly exchanging smiles and sharing food. Samuel blushes bright red when she laughs at one of his jokes, and she responds with an even bigger laugh, her cheeks glowing. It's adorable to watch the sparks of puppy love forming.

Governor Bradford and Captain Standish raise their glasses in gracious toasts, acknowledging the blessing of the union. Around us, the air is full of joy, music, and the sounds of children playing, delighting in the celebration.

Laughter and music ripple through the air as some of the Wampanoag play their drums and sing, moving in rhythm, their dances lively and flowing. Tekoa shows Samuel the steps, and he mirrors her movements with a shy impishness. A few of the children join in, clapping along, while some of the adults watch hesitantly, unsure if they should participate.

I lean close to Danielle, whispering, "I think it's wonderful that they're bringing their culture to your wedding, even if not everyone seems to approve."

She nods, her eyes sparkling with delight as the joyful energy spreads through the evening. It's a celebration of union, friendship, and shared lives.

I take Isaac's hand as one of the Wampanoag begins a lively circle dance, and I can't help laughing as we follow along. The rhythm is infectious, and soon we're spinning and stepping in time with the others, letting ourselves get swept away by the music. Some of the settlers try the steps, too, hesitantly at first, while others simply watch, clapping along. I glance at Isaac, and he's grinning, completely caught up in the joy of the moment, and it makes my chest ache with affection.

When the song ends, voices in the crowd lift in approval, and I lean closer to him, my voice barely audible over the noise. "Would you… like to steal a moment, just the two of us?" I ask, hoping he feels the same pull I do.

He nods, a slow smile spreading across his face. "Aye. Of course I would," he whispers.

We walk past Danielle and Henry, offering quick congratulations, and then slip quietly away from the feast one at a time so if anyone notices, they won't think we left together. I catch up with Isaac near the clearing. The laughter and music fade behind us as we head toward his house, our hearts still racing, savoring the small, private thrill of being alone together amid the celebration.

We duck into his house, locking the door behind us. The fire in the hearth glows warmly, chasing away the sharp chill. He guides me further inside, moving closer, his hands brushing my arms, gentle but insistent. We move toward the bed in the corner, and I can feel his desire, his focus on me alone. His hand cups my cheek, tilting my face toward him, and I lean into him, closing my eyes, savoring the tension, the anticipation, the closeness.

Before I know it, we're undressed together in Isaac's bed. I feel his hands all over me as I mount him, and a thrill runs through me. I moan, feeling pleasure roll through every cell of my body. He feels so good, I can't even remember what I was worried about all day.

As I grind against him, he pulls me down to kiss my lips, squeezing my breasts. I love Isaac's rough, strong hands on my most sensitive skin. His kiss and the heat of his touch make the intensity of my feelings even stronger. Everything else ceases to exist for a moment, and we climax together.

We lie tangled afterward, the quiet of the room wrapping around us. My mind replays the day: the ceremony, Danielle's joy, the music, the dancing, but beneath it all, a restlessness twists inside me.

Part of me longs for home, for the world I know and understand, yet another part feels like it belongs here, with Isaac. I close my eyes, overwhelmed by being caught between two worlds and unsure where I truly belong.

MORE SENSE THAN FEAR

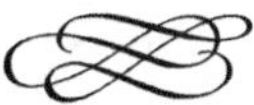

AFTER WE MADE LOVE LAST NIGHT, ALYSSA WENT BACK TO THE CONNOR house. We knew she couldn't stay here without risking everything. Alas, I had to let her go. How I wish she could stay with me all night, every night.

I lie in bed for a moment, wishing I could rewind time and keep her here just a little longer. Then a scream cuts through my reverie. I throw off the covers, swing my legs over the side of the bed, and grab my clothes.

Shouts echo through the settlement before I even reach the Connors' yard–dozens of angry voices, shouting words that make my stomach churn. I run.

By the time I reach the house, the scene is madness. Half the village is there, Priscilla, John Alden, Elder Brewster, even some of the older women, their faces twisted in fear and rage.

Alyssa is standing on the steps barefoot, her hair loose and wild in the wind. Two men have her by the arms, dragging her down like she's some criminal.

Priscilla's voice cuts through the crowd. "She's bewitched us! She brought the heathens among us! She danced with them, and she cursed our children!"

"She's no witch!" I roar, shoving through the bodies. The smell of smoke burns my throat. I see the woodpile forming in the square.

"Three children took fever in the night," John Alden bellows. "This is the devil's work, Owens! You know it!"

I plant myself in front of Alyssa, my hand on my knife. "Let her go!"

Alyssa's face is streaked with dirt and tears, but she lifts her chin. "People dance at weddings in nearly every culture," she says, her voice shaking but strong. "And no one has ever been harmed by it! Let me help the sick people rather than spending our morning spreading fear!"

Her words only fuel them. "Blasphemy!" someone shouts. "She mocks us still!"

Two men start toward me. "Stand aside, Owens," Alden warns. "You'd defend a witch?"

I swing before he finishes. My fist connects with his jaw, and he goes down hard. The other man lunges. I meet him with a shove that sends him sprawling into the dust. The crowd gasps but doesn't scatter. The men holding Alyssa's arms let go in shock.

"Mistress Montgomery, go inside!" I shout, but someone's already dragging her toward the fire again. She screams, kicking free long enough for me to grab her wrist. I pull her behind me, pushing through the crush of bodies.

"Danielle!" I hear Henry shouting nearby, his voice raw. He's trying to get to his wife, who's cornered near the fence while men wave torches. Henry throws one of them to the ground, snarling like a man possessed.

The crowd is splitting, half toward the Connors' house, half toward the Lewis house. Smoke thickens as someone lights a bundle of straw.

"Isaac, they'll kill us," Alyssa whispers.

"I'll protect you. Don't worry."

Another man lunges. I drive my shoulder into his chest, sending him reeling. "Get back!" I shout to the rest. "You touch her again and I'll lay you all out!"

Then a child screams somewhere behind the crowd, and I know the madness is only just beginning.

Henry's roar cuts through the mob. "Step away from my wife!" And I see him slam a man backward into the dirt. Another swings at him, and Henry meets the blow with his fist. His jaw cracks like dry wood. Danielle's sobbing, clutching her arm where someone struck her. Alyssa screams as a woman yanks her hair, dragging her toward the flames again.

I grab the woman's arm and twist until she lets go. "You touch her again, I'll break your hand," I snarl.

Alyssa stumbles back against me, shaking, her cheek bleeding where someone struck her.

The crowd's roar swells, shouts of "Burn the witches!" and "Send them back to hell!"

A torch flies past us and hits the ground, scattering sparks.

Then a deep voice booms over the madness. "Enough!"

Everyone freezes. Governor Bradford stands on the edge of the crowd, his face red with fury, and beside him is Captain Standish, his hand on his sword.

"Put out your torches!" Standish bellows. "You shame yourselves before God!"

The mob hesitates, but the authority in his voice cuts through their frenzy. Men lower their torches, still fuming.

Bradford strides forward, his cloak snapping in the wind. "You call these women witches while you riot like heathens yourselves?" His voice is sharp as flint. "If there is guilt, it will be decided in the meetinghouse, not in the street!"

No one dares argue. The fire crackles lower as the crowd moves toward their homes, some still shouting, others silent and shaken. Henry pulls Danielle into his arms. I keep my arm around Alyssa, leading her toward the meetinghouse with the rest.

Inside, the air is heavy and hot, thick with anger and fear. The benches fill fast. Those who want Alyssa and Danielle burned sit on one side, their faces tight with conviction. The others, fewer but braver, sit opposite. Among them are Thomas and Ann Tinker, and of course, Samuel.

Bradford stands at the front beside Standish. "Each will speak in turn," Bradford says. "And God will hear what is just."

One by one, they stand. Priscilla first, her eyes bright with righteousness. "The sickness is no coincidence," she declares. "Three children have fevers after the heathen dance. Mistress Montgomery and the Lewis family brought the devil into our midst!" Murmurs of agreement ripple through her side.

Goodman Brewster rises next. "Aye, my own boy vomited blood before dawn," he says, his voice cracking. "We were cursed the moment those savages touched our soil."

Each word grates against my chest. Alyssa sits still beside me, her hands folded.

When Bradford finally turns to her, the room quiets. "Mistress Montgomery," he says. "You may speak."

She rises slowly. Every eye follows her. "You all waste time sitting here while your children lie sick," she says. "You call me witch, but you forget it was Danielle and me who tended the Connor children when they were dying. We saw them rise from their deathbeds healthier than they'd ever been. They are now the healthiest children in the village."

She steps forward, her eyes brimming with tears. "Maybe your children wouldn't be sick if you spent more time gathering, hunting, and cooking, and less time gossiping."

Gasps ripple through the room. Bradford's brow furrows, but Alyssa doesn't stop. "I'm going to tend to the sick," she says coldly. "Anyone with more sense than fear is welcome to help."

She turns and walks toward the door, every step clicking in the stunned silence. Alyssa's hand is on the meetinghouse door when Bradford's voice stops her.

"Mistress Montgomery…."

She turns slowly. Her chin lifts, defiant, ready for judgment, but Bradford's expression isn't of anger. "Please," he says quietly. "Help us."

The words hang in the air like a bell. No one breathes.

Then Alyssa nods once. "Very well," she says. She strides back to the front, every inch of her calm, though her hair is tangled and there's blood on her cheek. "We'll need everyone's hands if we're to stop this sickness before it spreads further."

The same men who called her witch a moment ago now listen, hesitant, uncertain.

Alyssa turns to them like a commander on a battlefield. "You, take a group to the river and fish. Bring back whatever you can catch by midday. Fresh food will do more good than panic."

A few men rise, glancing toward Bradford, who gives a silent nod. They file out without a word.

"Goody Tinker," Alyssa continues. "Gather the women and go to the woods north of the clearing. There are herbs that will break fever: wintergreen, willow bark, and feverfew. Please bring back every sprig you can find."

Goody Tinker rises without hesitation, Samuel following close behind her.

Alyssa moves next to the hearth, gesturing toward a group of men still seated near the back. "The rest of you should start fires near the green and start boiling water. We'll need broth and clean water boiling by the hour."

She's moving fast now, and they're all following like the tide pulled by the moon.

Then Priscilla stands, her face blotched red. "This is foolishness," she spits. "You think we'll take orders from a woman!"

Standish steps forward, his boots echoing against the floorboards. "Priscilla Mullins," he says, his tone cold as steel, "if I hear one more word out of your mouth, you'll be the one we build the fire for."

The color drains from her face. She sits without a sound.

Alyssa doesn't even look at her. She simply nods once to Standish and then turns back to the crowd. "If we work together, the children will see the sunrise tomorrow. If we don't—" Her voice falters for just a heartbeat but then steadies again. "Then God forgive us all."

The meetinghouse empties quickly after that, boots on the ground, the clatter of tools and baskets, voices hushed but urgent. I stay where I am, just watching her.

Moments ago, she was fighting for her life, bleeding, and about to be burned at the stake. Now she commands them like she's been doing it her whole life. Bradford stands beside her, listening to every word, and even Standish looks at her with respect.

I can't move or speak. I can only watch in awe. The woman they tried to destroy just offered to help save them, and I love her even more for it.

LIFE IS SHORT

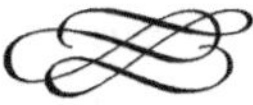

Alyssa

I press a damp cloth to the cut on my cheek, wincing at the sting. The bruises along my arms throb every time I move, reminders of this morning. I can still see the angry faces, hear the screams, feel the sparks flying too close to my hair, the pulling, the shoving, the heat of the torches, and the terror that nearly made me collapse. Every time I blink, I see them trying to drag me toward the fire. My stomach twists in knots just remembering it.

Now, I sit at the small kitchen table in Henry and Danielle's house, my hands folded over my tea, feeling every ache and twinge of pain in my body. Henry sits across from Danielle, both quiet, watching me with concern but careful not to crowd me. Isaac sits near the hearth, his arms crossed, his dark eyes on me.

"Even with all your care, some of the Tinkers and more children are starting to show symptoms now," Danielle says. "Actually, I'm not feeling too well myself. I hope I'm just tired."

I nod. Even after hours of tending, the sickness is spreading faster than we can keep up with. I sip my tea carefully, wishing it could soothe more than my throat.

"Mistress Montgomery," Henry says. "It's your life that I fear for most of all. I have spoken to the leaders and confirmed that now that Danielle is my wife, she will be protected. The villagers don't see her as outspoken as you. They have put the mark of the Lord's judgment on you, and something like that would take a miracle to outlive."

I look down at my hands. "Every day I stay here," I whisper, "it makes me want to go home more. I don't want to leave the three of you, but I can't stay, not with some of these people watching, waiting, hoping I'll slip up. They blame me for anything and everything that goes wrong here."

Isaac moves closer, sitting at the table beside me, and I feel the weight of his concern pressing against me. I hate that I can't just lean on him, that I have to consider leaving when I love him so much.

"I want to stay with all of you," I admit, my voice trembling. "I want to be here, safe with you, but I also know I can't. Every moment I do, I risk being dragged into the fire again. Even though they're letting me help now, it feels like only a matter of time before they try to take my life again, and what if the governor doesn't step in next time? What if he gives up on helping me? He has made no such promise for me."

Henry tightens his jaw, Danielle bites her lip, and Isaac's expression hardens. He doesn't argue. He knows what I said is true. This village has had it out for me since I arrived.

I take another sip of tea, trying to steady my trembling hands. Even here, inside this quiet kitchen, the memory of the flames and screaming clings to me. I close my eyes, wishing desperately that I could stay, yet knowing in my heart that I can't.

I push my chair back from the table and pick up a small pot of warm broth Danielle's been heating. "I'm going to check on the Tinkers before I return to the Connor children," I say, trying to keep my voice calm. "I just want to make sure they're all right."

The walk to the Tinker house is quiet. I pause at their door, inhaling the cool morning air before knocking. Samuel answers the door, and I step inside. Dawn's light slices across the floorboards, illuminating Mr. and Mrs. Tinker lying pale and weak in their bed. Their brows glisten with sweat, and their bodies shiver despite the blankets.

I set down the pot and kneel beside them. "I wanted to thank you," I murmur softly. "Thank you for helping all night and for working with me to care for the children and the sick. I'm sorry you're feeling this way now." My voice catches. "I think you might have something very contagious." Their eyes fill with confusion, and I quickly add, "Er, it means it can spread easily from one person to another. I think it might be typhoid fever. That's why you're so weak and feverish. We'll do what we can to get you healthy again."

I help them sip the warm broth out of cups, slowly, making sure they are able to swallow comfortably. Their breathing eases, just a little, and I press a cool cloth to Mrs. Tinker's forehead.

When I'm satisfied that they're stable for the moment, I rise and move over to the small table where Samuel sits, his knees drawn up, staring at the floor. "Samuel," I say gently, "you need to take care of yourself, too. Check on your parents, but remember to rest, eat what you can, and keep your strength up."

He looks up at me, a smile tugging at his lips. "I will," he says but then pauses, his eyes brightening. "Mistress Montgomery, I've been thinking today about the future, about plans, dreams. It just seems like life is very short."

"You're right about that, my friend. Tell me, what are your plans and dreams?"

"Well, I'm thinking I'll ask Tekoa to be my wife someday."

I look at him in surprise. Wife? They're barely more than children, but then I remember: it's 1621. Fifteen is old enough to get married and have children here. I let out a soft laugh. "You can do anything you want, Samuel," I say, smiling. "You're a good child—no, a good man."

His face brightens. "Man?" he whispers.

"Yes," I say firmly. "A man who can care for his family, protect them, and still follow his heart."

He beams, pride lighting his eyes. I kneel beside him, showing him how to check his parents' pulses, how to keep them hydrated, and how to notice if their fever rises. "If they get worse at any time, even in the middle of the night, come and find me. I'll help."

"I will," he promises.

I rise, brushing my hands together, and step into the cool morning air, heading back to the Connor house. The quiet is almost oppressive. Once inside, I wash my hands, arms, and face thoroughly, determined not to carry typhoid to them. I tidy the small kitchen, preparing their simple meal and then watch the Connor children eat, laughing and chattering, blissfully unaware of the danger others have faced today.

And still, my chest aches. I've risked everything to help, faced fire and mobs, and yet, some villagers still think I'm the victim.

I love Isaac. I will miss Danielle every second I'm home without her. I care deeply for the children here, but the longing in my chest for home is stronger than anything. Every day I remain reminds me of the world I left behind and how I simply do not fit in here.

The day is spent caring for the sick, mostly inside the Connor house because I want to stay away from those who tried to harm me last night. Isaac and the others bring me herbs and food to cook and then deliver it to the sick.

Later that evening, I tuck the children in, checking their small faces for fever one last time. I love them all, but more than anything, right now, I want to go home.

I sit for a moment, letting the quiet settle around me. The day has left its mark, bruises, cuts, and exhaustion. Danielle and I aren't worried about typhoid ourselves. We've been vaccinated. But she's clearly spent, and I can't help worrying about her. I'm scared that Isaac or Henry might catch it, and the thought knocks the wind out of me.

All I can do is make sure that everyone rests as best they can, drinks clean water, and eats nourishing food. Amid all the care, the chaos, and the fear, all I can think is how badly I want to go home.

SICKNESS

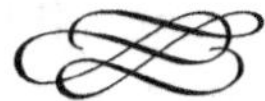

Mist hangs low over the fields, swallowing sound, and my breath curls white in the air as I step outside. I head for the Connors' house to help Alyssa with the children's breakfast, but when I knock, Danielle opens the door instead. She looks tired, and her hands are still dusted with flour.

"Good morrow, Goody Lewis. I came to help Alyssa with breakfast."

"Good morning. Thank you for calling me Goody Lewis," she beams. "That's one of the first times anyone's said that, and it makes me feel like such a proper wife. Oh, but Alyssa isn't here."

"Not here?"

"She went to check on the Tinkers earlier. She said she'd be back before the little ones woke."

"I'll go see if I can lend her a hand there then, if you don't need my help here?"

"Henry's inside helping fry the fish and bake the bread. I'm sure Alyssa would appreciate the company. Just try not to get sick."

I nod and bid her farewell. As I enter the Tinker yard, I notice their front door is ajar.

"Alyssa?" I call from the porch.

There's no answer.

When I step inside, the stale air hits me, heavy with sickness. Alyssa is kneeling on the floor next to a bed. Samuel Tinker lies still, his face as pale as the linen shirt clinging to him.

She looks up, her eyes red and glistening. "Isaac," she whispers. "They're gone."

My stomach twists into a knot. I look to the other beds. Thomas and Jane Tinker lie side by side, their faces also pale, their chests still.

I run to Alyssa, my knees hitting the floor beside Samuel's outstretched arm. He's fourteen, nearly grown, strong-shouldered from chopping wood. Seeing him like this steals the breath from my lungs.

Alyssa strokes his hair with shaking fingers. "He wasn't breathing when I got here," she says, her voice cracking. "I didn't realize he was sick last night. He was smiling, laughing even... talking about how he wanted to marry Tekoa. I should've stayed...."

I shake my head. "You did all you could. You didn't know they were this sick. They were helping us yesterday, and they seemed to be doing well compared to everyone else we helped."

She presses her lips together hard as if to stop herself from crying again. "He was so proud of helping yesterday," she whispers.

I swallow the ache in my throat. "He was a good boy," I say quietly. "They were good people. We'll make sure they're buried properly," I say. "And that everyone knows what they did for the village."

She nods faintly, wiping her face with her sleeve. "They didn't deserve this."

"No," I murmur, my eyes burning. "No one does."

She leans into me, and I wrap my arm around her shoulders. For a while we just kneel there, surrounded by the quiet.

Later that evening, after Henry, John, and I have dug the Tinkers' graves, everyone meets to pay their respects. I look out across a blanket of sorrowful faces and notice that even the gulls circling over the bay seem to cry softer, their voices muted against the low gray clouds. We gather together where the three freshly dug graves wait: Thomas, Jane, and young Samuel Tinker. The sight of them lined together makes me weep. Alyssa stands beside me, sobbing into her apron.

Elder Brewster's voice carries over the crowd, low and solemn. His words blur in my ears: mercy, rest, and eternal peace.

When the final "Amen" fades, the silence stretches too long. Then Goody Brewster speaks softly, her voice trembling. "Mistress Montgomery, Goody Lewis, would you sing for the Tinkers?"

Alyssa's head lifts slightly. Danielle touches her arm, and they step forward together. Alyssa glances at me, her eyes brimming with tears, and then she begins.

The sound that leaves her is so ethereal, it doesn't belong in this cold place. It's not a hymn or psalm. It's something entirely new. The melody is simple but strange, rising and falling like breath. Danielle joins in, her softer voice weaving around Alyssa's. The two of them sound like hope and heartbreak mixed together, and I swear the whole world pauses to listen.

It's a gentle song, threading through the air like a whisper of comfort in the dark. Their voices melt together in harmony, and there's a line speaking of Mary, the mother of Jesus, offering quiet guidance and solace, and another that promises, even in the shadow of anguish, there will be an answer. The message is patient and tender, carrying a single, simple truth: sometimes, we must let things be as they are. The crowd listens, their faces softening, and even the men who usually hide their hearts seem genuinely touched.

I feel it, too, a strange warmth in my chest, the kind of hope that seems impossible in the middle of mourning. Somewhere deep down, I know this song is meant to carry people through the worst of it, to remind them to breathe, to endure, as it says, to let things be.

Alyssa looks upward, tears sliding down her cheeks, her lips still trembling from the song. She's the strongest person I've ever known, and seeing her so broken shatters something inside me. I can't look at her without wanting to pull her close and promise her she'll never hurt like this again.

After the burial, the crowd disperses slowly. I walk with Alyssa back toward the Connor house. Neither of us speaks. What words could possibly make this better?

When we reach the door, the Connor children rush toward her, their laughter cutting through the heaviness like sunlight through clouds. Alyssa forces a tight smile, kneeling to hug them, her voice warm and gentle as she asks about their day. I help her cook them dinner, and afterward, the children run outside to play. The fire crackles low. Alyssa sets her bowl aside and rubs her temples, her eyes tired and distant. I move closer, resting a hand on her shoulder.

"You sing so beautifully," I say quietly. "And the way you care for these children even when you are in pain is nothing short of heroic."

She shakes her head. "I'm no hero."

"You are," I tell her, and I mean it. "You care for everyone else first."

Her eyes meet mine, and for a moment, the grief between us eases. I reach up, brush a tear from her cheek, and then I gently kiss her lips. Even in the midst of loss, she feels like the only warmth in a world gone cold.

When the children file back inside, and the fire burns low, the sky outside deepens into twilight. Alyssa sits close beside me, her fingers wrapped around a mug of tea. She hasn't said much since the burial, though I can tell her thoughts haven't stopped for a moment.

A knock sounds at the door, and I rise to open it. Henry and Danielle step inside, their faces drawn and weary from the day's tribulation. Danielle carries a basket with bread and greens, and Henry follows with a stack of firewood.

"We thought some company might do us all good," Henry says softly.

Alyssa manages a small smile. "The tea's still warm," she murmurs, rising to find more cups.

We sit together around the small table. The Connor children have gone to bed in the loft above us. It feels strange to be speaking of anything other than woe, but after a few minutes, the conversation shifts to the practical, the kind of talk that has to happen whether hearts are ready or not.

Henry clears his throat. "We need to decide what'll happen to these children," he says before pausing, glancing at Alyssa. "If you go home."

Her hand stills on her cup. She nods once, eyes on the table. "I was going to ask the Tinkers to care for them," she says quietly. "They were good with the children, but now…."

Her voice trails off, and none of us need her to finish.

Danielle reaches over, touching Alyssa's hand. "Henry and I have talked," she says. "If you do decide to return to our time, we'll take them in. We'll build on another room, and they already know us."

Alyssa's eyes soften with relief. "Thank you," she whispers. "Taking that worry off the table means more than you know."

Danielle starts to stand, then her face goes pale, her hand trembling against her cup. "I—"

"Danielle?" Henry moves fast, catching her before she hits the floor. Her eyelids flutter and then close. Alyssa rushes around the table, grabbing a cloth and soaking it in the washbasin.

"Lay her in my bed," Alyssa says quickly, her voice calm but tight with worry. Henry and I ease Danielle onto the small bed near the hearth. Alyssa presses the cool cloth to her forehead, her other hand on her throat.

"Her heart's racing," she murmurs. "Please, get her some water."

Alyssa removes Danielle's cap to cool her head more quickly. Finally, Danielle opens her eyes and looks up at Henry, confused but awake.

"What happened?" she whispers.

"You fainted," Alyssa says softly, brushing hair from her face. "You're overheated and probably exhausted. You've been running yourself ragged."

Henry strokes his wife's hand, his jaw tight. "Is it the sickness?"

Alyssa shakes her head. "No, it can't be typhoid fever. We've both been vaccinated against it."

Henry frowns. "Vaccinated?"

I glance between them. "What does that mean?"

Alyssa looks up at me. "It means we were given medicine in our time that protects us from certain illnesses," she explains. "It helps the body fight off diseases before they ever take hold."

Henry stares, clearly trying to grasp the idea. I can't blame him. My mind reels. "You're saying your people can stop sickness before it begins?" I ask, astonished.

She nods. "Some of them, yes. Illnesses that kill people in this time, like typhoid and smallpox, are preventable in the future."

When Danielle's breathing steadies, Alyssa wrings out the cloth again and lays it over her friend's brow.

The sight of them, Alyssa bending over Danielle, both women far too brave for the dangers that surround them, knots something deep inside me. I think of the mob, the sickness sweeping through the village, and the graves in the wet earth. Alyssa and Danielle don't belong here. This place will swallow them if it can.

When Henry finally thanks Alyssa for her help and carries Danielle home, the house falls silent again. I stand by the hearth, watching Alyssa gather the empty cups, her shoulders bowed with fatigue.

She's tired, too worn, yet still she moves with purpose, always fighting to heal, comfort and protect.

I reach out, catching her hand before she can move away. "You did it again tonight," I tell her quietly. "You take care of everyone like an angel."

"I'm no angel. I just hope Danielle's all right."

"She will be," I say, though part of me doubts my words.

As she leans into me, I look into the fire and think of what she told us about her time and the medicine. That's where she belongs. That's where Danielle belongs, too.

I wonder if sending them both home, away from sickness and sorrow, might be the only way to truly do what is right.

NOT A HEALER

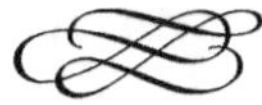

Alyssa

I scrub the last of the breakfast dishes clean. The Connors' kitchen smells of bread and fried fish, the comforting kind of ordinary that feels almost out of place after so much loss. I dry my hands on a cloth, glance toward the children playing, and tell them I'm going to check on Danielle. They nod, and I wrap my shawl tighter before stepping out into the cool air.

The path to the Lewis house is muddy, and my boots squelch in the soft earth. A few women hang laundry on the line, and I catch the faint murmur of a prayer drifting from an open window. When I reach the door, I knock softly. Henry opens it a moment later, his eyes weary.

"Is she awake?" I ask.

He nods, motioning me inside. "Aye, but still not herself. She's been sick since last night."

The room is warm and dim, the air thick with the scent of herbs and firewood. Danielle lies in bed, her face pale against the pillow, her hair unpinned and falling loose around her shoulders. She manages a tired smile when she sees me.

"How are you feeling?"

"I can't keep anything down," she says softly. "If I could, I think I'd feel better."

Henry brings a steaming cup of tea to her bedside, and she takes it from him carefully, testing the temperature before sipping.

"Mint. It'll help settle your stomach," he says.

"I'm just tired," she murmurs. "And dizzy whenever I stand. My stomach's been turning all morning."

I sit beside her, watching her face for clues. "Any fever? Chills? Pain anywhere?"

She shakes her head. "No fever. Just everything feels like it's spinning, and I can't seem to keep much food down."

Henry frowns, crossing his arms. "She nearly fainted again when she tried to help with the bread."

"Then she shouldn't be helping with the bread," I say gently, giving her a warning look.

Danielle leans her head back, her eyes closing for a moment. "It feels odd not to help. Plus, it's probably just exhaustion," she says. "We've all been running too much these last few days."

"Maybe," I answer softly, though I'm not entirely convinced. "You've been pushing too hard. Your body's asking you to stop for a little while."

She smiles faintly. "Yes, Mother."

"Don't 'yes, Mother' me, young lady. I'll ground you to your bed for a month."

"Don't threaten me with a good time," she says with a grin.

Henry chuckles under his breath, the sound a rare comfort in the small room. He ladles broth into a bowl, but before he can hand it to Danielle, there's a sharp knock on the door.

Henry moves to open it, and there stands John Alden. His face is flushed, his breath ragged from running.

"Mistress Montgomery," he says, gripping the frame as if to steady himself. "I'm glad I found you here. Please, come quickly. Mistress

Mullins has been bit by something fierce, and she won't listen to sense. It's deep in her arm, and she's burning with fever."

My stomach drops. "By what?"

"I don't know," he says. "Yesterday, she cried out, then I saw a welt rising like fire under her skin."

I grab my satchel. "Show me."

We hurry down the path toward the Mullins' house, John moving fast despite the slick ground. His voice breaks as he says, "She wouldn't let me fetch anyone. Wouldn't let me help her, but she's shaking now, and…." He swallows hard. "Please, you must help her."

Priscilla lies on the bed, her cheeks flushed, her lips pale. She's trembling, and sweat drips down her forehead. The swelling on her forearm is awful, angry red rivers spreading outward, with a dark, bluish center where the skin has started to sink, with two faint puncture marks the middle. My instincts kick into high gear.

"Priscilla," I whisper, kneeling beside her. "Can you tell me when this happened?"

She grimaces. "Last morning. Felt a sting while I was hanging the linens. Now, I can't breathe."

"You've been bitten by a brown recluse spider. Its venom can destroy tissue, and infection comes fast."

"Infection?"

"An infection is the way you are feeling right now. It's coming from the poison in your blood," I reply. Then I turn to John. "Please bring me water and something to boil it in, and I need bandages."

He bolts out the door without a word.

I crush a few willow leaves from my satchel for pain relief. It's a natural form of aspirin, and I set them to steep in hot water when John returns. I mix honey and crushed garlic for an antiseptic paste, spreading it lightly around the wound to keep infection at bay. "This will sting," I warn her.

She nods and closes her eyes tightly. "It already burns worse than fire."

When the paste is in place, I give her a small dose of willow tea. "This will help with the pain and fever. Keep drinking, slowly." Then, I cover the wound with a clean bandage. "You'll need to rest and keep it clean. No scratching. No handling anything heavy till the swelling eases."

Priscilla blinks up at me, her eyes glassy. "I thought you were strange, Mistress Montgomery, speaking of things no one understands, but you've saved me." Her voice cracks. "I'm sorry for the words I said before. I was frightened of what I didn't know."

I squeeze her hand. "There's nothing to forgive. You'll heal, Mistress Mullins. I promise."

John lets out a long breath, his shoulders sagging. "Thank you," he says softly. "I didn't know who else could help."

"Just keep her cool," I tell him. "If the fever worsens, send for me right away."

As I step back into the sunlight, I realize my hands are still trembling. One bite from a tiny spider, and it could've taken her life.

I drag my feet along the dirt path, my thoughts still tangled with Priscilla's fever and the memory of that wound. Every time I see someone sick or hurt here, I'm reminded of how fragile everything is, how a single insect bite could take a life.

I'm halfway to the Lewis house when I spot Isaac coming toward me, his stride quick. His hair is tied back, but the wind blows strands across his forehead. When he sees me, he gives a tired smile.

"I was just coming to find you," he says. "I wondered if you might join me at my house? I wish to speak with you."

I agree, and we walk the path together. The trees rustle overhead, scattering a few leaves that drift down like flecks of copper. When we reach his house, the fire's already burning.

He pours two cups of tea and clears his throat. "Alyssa," he begins, his eyes fixed on the table, "I've been thinking about you. Indeed, I think about you all the time. I pray for you, and us, and I wonder…."

"Isaac—"

He shakes his head gently. "I know, I'm babbling, but please. Let me finish." His gaze lifts to mine, and he looks almost distraught. "You've done so much good here, but this place is dangerous. There's no medicine like you have in your own time, not the kind you're used to. You come from a world that can heal what we can't. I can't bear the thought of something happening to you here when you might live free and whole where you came from with comforts I can't even fathom, with safety I can't provide."

His words cut deep because I know they're true. "You think I should go back?" I whisper.

He nods, his jaw tightening. "Even though it feels like tearing something out of me to say it."

I stare into my cup. "As much as I love you, Isaac… I think you're right." My voice trembles, but I force the words out. "I was never meant to be a healer or a nurse. I'm a teacher. That's who I am. And I miss my family more than I ever thought I could. Every day here feels borrowed."

"Then how do we send you back?"

"I don't know," I admit. "But I think I know who might." I set the cup down, meeting his eyes. "Tekoa's grandmother, Kesuk. She's a healer, but more than that, she understands things we don't and speaks with the spirits. Danielle and I have approached her before about this, and she said one of us will go, but she was vague. Maybe she will have more guidance now that I am in clear danger here."

Isaac nods slowly. "Then, we'll go speak with her."

The trail to the Wampanoag camp is quiet except for the crunch of frost beneath our boots. Isaac walks beside me, silent, his brow furrowed in thought. Neither of us has said much since leaving the village, but I know we're both turning over the same questions: how, when, and if I'm meant to return to my own time.

When we near the edge of the settlement, a group of women bend over a line of drying venison, and an older man waves when he recognizes Isaac.

Tekoa steps out from behind a hut, a bow slung over her shoulder. Her eyes brighten when she sees us. "Isaac, Alyssa," she says. "What brings you here?"

"We were hoping to speak with your grandmother again, if she's available."

Tekoa nods, though a trace of curiosity flickers in her expression. "She rests this morning, but I will take you."

She leads us through the camp toward the lodge near the far end. A few familiar faces glance up as we pass. Samoset is among them. He's mending a fishing net near the fire. "Mistress Montgomery," he says with a nod. "Always walking with purpose."

"Good day, Samoset. Purpose? I'm certainly trying," I answer, and he smiles and greets Isaac too before returning to his work.

Tekoa gestures for us to wait by the doorway of Kesuk's lodge. "I will tell her you have come," she says, stepping inside.

The moment stretches uncomfortably, and Isaac glances around anxiously. I feel a sense that something irreversible is waiting on the other side of this conversation.

When Tekoa returns, she holds the flap open. "She will see you now."

Inside, the air is warm from a small fire. Dried herbs hang in bundles overhead. Kesuk sits cross-legged near the flames, her posture straight despite her years, her eyes half-closed as if she's already been listening to a question I haven't asked yet.

I lower myself onto the mat across from her. "I need your guidance," I say softly. "I need to know exactly how to return to my own time, and whether it is me who will return there or Danielle."

Tekoa translates. Kesuk doesn't answer right away. She closes her eyes, murmuring low and rhythmically under her breath. The air in the lodge seems to shift, charged with something unseen.

Finally, she speaks. Tekoa's tone changes, slower now. "She says the spirits are restless. The path that once was clear has changed. It is no longer meant for one."

"Does she mean that what she said before has changed?"

"Two will return," Tekoa says slowly, her voice low. "Love binds them. With the guidance of two, they will cross the water and be carried safely. The new bride carries life within her."

My stomach drops. I look at Isaac, then back at Tekoa. "The new bride?"

It hits me all at once.

"She's not ill," I whisper. "She's pregnant."

Kesuk opens her eyes, watching me with a knowing calm that sends a shiver through me. I realize the spirits have spoken, and not about me, but about who truly needs to go home.

We turn to Kesuk, and I bow my head, my voice low. "Thank you, Kesuk, for everything. Your guidance means more than words can say."

Isaac nods beside me, adding his own quiet thanks. Tekoa translates them, and Kesuk's eyes shine. I reach out to touch her hand. "Goodbye," I whisper, and she squeezes my hand, a gesture full of warmth and farewell. Tekoa steps back, letting us go, and we start down the path, our hearts heavy but grateful for the wisdom she's shared.

Tekoa leads us a short way down the path until we meet Samoset, still sitting near the fire. When Tekoa returns to her grandmother, Isaac and I exchange a glance.

"Samoset?" I begin, my voice catching. "There's something we need you to tell Tekoa." I swallow hard and press on. "The boy, young Samuel Tinker, has passed away. He had a very high fever and never recovered. Please tell Tekoa. They were friends."

Samoset listens carefully, the gravity of what we've said sinking in, and he promises he will tell her.

As we start back down the path toward home, the first cries pierce the quiet. Tekoa's voice, raw, wild, and unrelenting, cuts through the forest.

I squeeze Isaac's hand, and he wraps his arm around me. I lean into him, letting the tremor of grief shake through me as her sobs echo through the woods. I understand, more than I ever thought I could. It's the helpless, aching sorrow of losing someone one cares for when there was nothing anyone could do. In the end, that will eat away at a person from within for years.

Isaac and I hold each other, our hearts breaking in shared mourning. I cry for Samuel, for Tekoa, for the home I won't see again, and all around us, the world seems to sag under sorrow.

STAY WITH ME

Alyssa

Isaac's hand is comforting around mine as we walk through the woods, the quiet between us full and easy. For a few stolen moments, we can ignore the rules of this time, while the judging eyes of the village, the whispers that would follow if we were seen like this, are too far off to see us. I loathe the rules of this era. People should be able to hold hands without shame. I despise the way they use religion for fear rather than love.

Our affectionate moment ends the instant the trees thin, and the village comes into view. We have to let go, our fingers slipping apart as if by command.

My stomach rolls over when I think of what Kesuk told us. Two will return. Love binds them. I'm never going home....

When we reach the Lewis house, Henry opens the door. Danielle sits by the fire, pale but smiling.

I don't waste a second. "Danielle," I say, breathless. "We visited the healer—Kesuk—and she gave me a message. You're not sick. You're going to have a baby!"

Danielle gasps. "A baby?" she whispers. "I—well, I suppose I am late." Her hand drifts to her stomach, trembling. "Oh, Henry!"

Her husband's mouth opens and closes like a man struck speechless. "You're certain?"

"As certain as I can be," I say, my smile soft and sure. "It does make sense, though, doesn't it?" I ask, turning back to Danielle. "Morning sickness, nausea, and lightheadedness."

"Yes, you're absolutely right. I can't believe we didn't realize it before." She lets out a small laugh—half disbelief and half joy. "A baby!"

Henry laughs, too. It's a shaky, broken sound. "I think I may be lightheaded at this point as well." He sinks into the nearest chair. "A child."

Isaac grins. "Congratulations, both of you."

Henry looks up, his eyes bright and wet. "Thank you, Isaac. I hardly know what to say."

"Sit for a spell," Isaac says gently. "You look as though you've seen a ghost."

Danielle laughs, light and musical, and I can't help smiling either. "Let's make something to eat," I suggest. "You two need food before you fall over."

Isaac and I move about the kitchen together, creating a melody through the scrape of pans, the crackle of the fire, and the rhythm of working side by side.

When we've all eaten, and the shock settles, Danielle looks at me curiously. "What did Kesuk say about you returning home?"

My smile fades. "That's the part I've been dreading telling you, Danielle. It's about you, and I know neither of you are going to like it."

Henry stiffens. "What did she say?"

"She said two will return," I answer quietly. "That love binds them, and that the new bride carries life within her."

Danielle stares at me, her lips parted. "I'm going to return... with my baby?"

I nod again, my throat tight. "The way she said it implied that it was for medical benefit or for the sake of safety. Something has changed, and two will go now, so I believe she means you and the baby."

Henry's chair scrapes the floor as he stands. "No. No, that's not possible. Danielle, please don't leave me."

Tears fill Danielle's eyes. "I don't want to."

I reach across the table, taking her hand. "I'm so sorry. I wish I could change it."

She swallows hard. "Then what about you?"

"I'll stay," I say softly. "I would make three, so that won't work. If it's so that you can safely have your baby, I'll stay."

The room falls quiet, firelight flickering over the four of us. When Isaac and I step outside, dusk has fallen. I don't speak right away, just walk beside him, my arms folded against the chill. My heart is filled with joy for Danielle and sorrow for myself.

"You did well back there," he says. "That couldn't have been easy to say."

I shake my head. "I think I just broke their hearts."

"Perhaps," he admits. "But they still have some time left together."

We reach the Connors' home, with the children's laughter soaring out through the cracks in the door, loud and wild. I smile and glance at Isaac. "Let's get these monkeys fed."

Inside, we move through the small kitchen, me stirring soup, him slicing bread. I find myself stealing glances at him every chance I get— his gorgeous face lit up by firelight, the way he can make even the simplest task seem masculine and sexy. I notice how his voice is gentler when he speaks to the children.

When the little ones finish their meal, we tuck them into bed, whispering goodnight as their breathing evens out. The house grows still, the fire burning low.

I gather the bowls, sighing as I wipe my hands. "It's strange… how much this place feels like home now," I murmur.

"It's because you made it so," Isaac says, his voice rougher than usual.

I turn, surprised, as he steps closer. "Alyssa, these past months, I've watched you put yourself aside for others. You've made this place better. You've made me better."

"Isaac...."

"When I thought you might leave, it felt as though the ground beneath me would give way, but now, knowing you'll stay, I can't imagine another dawn without you."

I gasp, covering my mouth with my hands. "What are you saying?"

He reaches for my hand. "I'm saying that I love you, Alyssa Montgomery. Stay with me, and be my wife."

I drop my hands to his shoulders, my eyes filling with tears. "Yes. Of course, yes." I fall into his arms. Our lips meet, and in his kiss, I feel reassurance, happiness, and love.

When he leaves a little later, the house feels too quiet. I stand by the window, watching his figure fade into the dark toward his house, which I suppose is soon to be my house.

I sit on the edge of the bed. This place, this period in time, is home now.

Danielle will get to go home to our time, and I'm going to be here, living and dying in a time that feels so foreign, where I feel so trapped. I'll make the best of it. I'll marry Isaac, and we'll raise the Connor kids together, and I'm sure I'll even find happiness in true love. But I'll never stop missing my family and my old life.

Jealousy creeps through me when I picture Danielle holding her baby, my mom showing her how to nurse, and my dad building a crib. Even James and Chloe will be happy to help with the baby.

I stretch out on the bed, staring up at the ceiling beams. I know this place now: the quiet after sundown, the sound of the waves, and the comfort of Isaac's voice. I love him so much, and I want to be his wife, and yet, my mind drifts.

Why me? Why did the universe, or God, or fate, whatever it is— pull me out of my time and drop me here? Why make me live a whole life in 2025 just to take it away? Why not just make me be born during this time instead?

Maybe it's because of the knowledge I've brought back with me, knowledge that has saved lives. But I will never know for sure.

The thoughts fade as my lids grow heavy. I pull the blanket higher, and before long, the hum of the wind outside lulls me to sleep.

WE MUST PRAY

WHEN SUNDAY'S CHURCH SERVICE CONCLUDES, THE PREACHER'S FINAL words trailing into the stillness of the meetinghouse, the congregation shifts, some standing, some staying in the pews.

I step forward, clearing my throat. "Friends and neighbors," I begin, my eyes sweeping over familiar faces. "Before you leave, I have an announcement." Heads turn, curiosity sharpening in their expressions. "Alyssa Montgomery and I are to be married." I've already spoken to the leaders, and they have blessed our upcoming union.

A ripple of surprise passes through the room. Then, gradually, nods and murmurs of congratulations spread. Relief warms me. They finally accept her. Across the aisle, our eyes meet. I hold her gaze, and she smiles at me, her green eyes shining in the sunlight.

I lift my voice again, eager to make the moment practical as well as joyful. "And I would ask, if any among you wish to join us tomorrow morning in the woods, to help hunt game for our wedding feast, you are welcome. It will be a jovial time."

Governor Bradford chuckles, tipping his head back. "Aye, that I will do. There's nothing better than a morning hunt."

Captain Standish grins. "Count me in, Owens."

The congregation disperses, most of the villagers stepping out into the crisp morning air. We fall in behind the Connor children as they hurry ahead toward their home, laughter filling the path.

Alyssa glances at the children and smiles. "The older boys can help seat everyone," she says, "and the younger girls can scatter petals along the aisle."

I nod, watching her delight in the small details of our wedding day, and we continue walking, keeping pace with the children as they chatter about the celebration to come.

We reach the Connor doorstep, and I pause. "I'll see you in the morning, and if you need anything before then, send for me."

She nods, thanks me, and steps inside. I watch her go and then turn and begin the walk home. My mind drifts ahead, imagining the days to come when Alyssa and the Connor children live in my house with me, our home filled with their joy and love.

I won't have to say goodbye to her anymore or leave her behind when night falls. She'll be mine, truly, and I'll be hers. The thought settles in my chest like a warm fire, blazing bright, and I can't help the wide, satisfied smile that spreads across my face.

THE NEXT MORNING, THE WINTER AIR BITES AT US. WE STEP OUT OF THE meetinghouse, the ground still damp from overnight frost. Bradford adjusts his musket, and Standish sharpens the edge of his knife with quiet precision. Alyssa walks beside me on one side, Henry on the other.

"Isaac, you think we'll see plenty of deer this morning?" Henry asks, glancing toward the woods.

"Aye," I reply, scanning the tree line. "And I trust Mistress Montgomery to guide us. She has a knack for knowing where they roam."

Alyssa grins, stepping ahead a little. "Deer follow patterns. They eat the same foods and are cautious of movement. We'll need to be quiet and methodical."

When we get to the ridge overlooking the valley, we fan out silently, moving through the underbrush, Alyssa at the center. She crouches, her eyes scanning the distant tree line, and I follow her gaze.

"There," she whispers. "See that? A herd will usually go down to graze in a valley before the sun gets high. We'll follow the line of pines and keep the wind in our favor. We don't want them to smell us."

Standish crouches beside her. "How do you know all this?"

"My grandfather taught me," she murmurs. "Deer sense the slightest movement, so step lightly. They also have a sharp sense of smell, so keep upwind. If we do it right, they won't even know we're near."

We creep along the slope, and I glance at her, marveling at her knowledge and confidence.

Finally, we crest a rise and spot them. A herd grazes in the meadow below, their ears flicking, their tails swishing lazily. I swallow hard. "There they are," I whisper.

Alyssa kneels, gesturing. "Do you see the largest buck? That one's cautious."

Henry swallows and nods, gripping his musket tightly. Bradford crouches low, and Standish mutters, "Quiet now."

One of the men fires. A sharp crack echoes, smoke curling from the barrel. The deer bolt. A flash of movement passes through the underbrush, then a scream.

I whirl toward Alyssa. Her hand clutches her arm, blood spreading across her sleeve. "Alyssa!" My voice breaks. She sways, collapsing to the ground.

"Mercy!" Bradford shouts. The men freeze, and I notice one of them in the back with a look of horror written across his face. It's clear he did not mean to hit Alyssa, but she was out in front of us a bit, and he must not have realized he didn't have a clean shot at the deer.

"She's hurt!" Henry exclaims, rushing forward.

I drop to my knees beside her. Her eyelids move rapidly as I lift her, blood soaking my hands. "Stay awake, Alyssa! Please, stay with me!" The wound seems to be in her chest, near her left shoulder.

"Isaac," she gasps, her voice weak.

"We need to get her back," I tell the others, my voice sharp.

I carry her through the forest, racing toward the village. Every step feels endless, her warm blood slipping through my fingers, her shallow breaths rattling against my ear.

By the time we reach the Lewis house, my chest burns, my legs ache, but I don't pause. I carry her through the doorway, calling for help. Danielle appears immediately, her eyes filled with horror at the sight of her friend drenched in blood.

"Lay her here!" she commands, and I place Alyssa gently on Danielle's bed. The sheets immediately darken from where she has bled through her clothing. Danielle grasps her hand, fear mirrored in her eyes.

Alyssa's eyes close and her body goes limp.

"Can we save her?"

Danielle shakes, frantic. "We must try!"

I press my hands over Alyssa's chest, holding the cloth tight as Danielle works swiftly. Her fingers trace the wound, her eyes sharp and focused. "The bleeding's slowing," she says, voice tense. "We've got it mostly under control, but the bullet is lodged deep in her shoulder."

I feel my stomach twist. "Will she—?" I choke out.

Danielle shakes her head. "She can survive if we care for her. She'll need hydration, nourishment, and rest, but the lead ball is lodged inside of her. It will need to be removed so it doesn't get infected."

"What will happen if it gets infected?"

Danielle sobs, and I feel my heart sink further with every tear that streams down her cheeks. "If it gets infected, her blood will become poisonous, and she won't live. It has to come out, or the infection will kill her."

I brush my thumb over Alyssa's cheek. "You're not leaving me," I whisper, though terror grips my chest.

Danielle binds the wound with clean cloths to slow the bleeding. "Stay calm," she urges. "We must pray."

Henry leans closer. "I'll go tell everyone to pray," he murmurs, rising. I hear him open the door, his footsteps fading.

Moments later, voices carry from outside. Standish's deep tone trembles. "I'm sorry, Owens... I—"

I press my face to Alyssa's, whispering every prayer I know. My bride-to-be lies still, her blood staining my hands, and all I can do is hold her and hope.

TIME TO GO

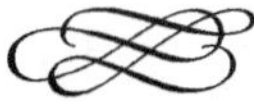

Heat envelopes me, and my chest throbs, sharp and burning. My head feels like it's splitting. I try to keep my eyes open and lift my head. Isaac sits in the chair beside me, asleep, his hands curled into a fists.

I try to move. Pain rips through my shoulder. I gasp, clutching it and tasting iron. The wound is wrapped in a bloody cloth, but I can feel the hole beneath, the bullet still lodged there.

Danielle's voice cuts through my thoughts. "Alyssa?" She runs to me, her eyes wide. "You're awake. Stay still."

"It hurts," I whisper.

"I know," she says, pressing her hand to my forehead, checking my fever. "We're keeping the bleeding down. Try not to move."

I force the words out. "The children... where are they? Who's watching them?"

Henry steps forward. "Priscilla Mullins is looking after them. They're safe."

Danielle lifts a small bowl. "Drink a little broth, just enough to keep you awake."

I sip, wincing, the dizzying fever crawling through me and turning my stomach over. My shoulder protests with every heartbeat.

"You're awake," Isaac says, stirring beside me. Relief floods his face, but fear lingers in his eyes.

Danielle tightens her fingers around mine. "Hold on. Breathe."

"It hurts so badly," I say. "I'm going to pass out again. Somebody needs to get me something stronger than broth."

There's a knock on the door, and Henry stands to open it.

I turn my head enough to see Moses Fletcher in the threshold. He steps carefully into the room, his eyes full of grief and guilt written across every line of his face. "Mistress Montgomery, I… I am so sorry. I don't know what happened. When I fired, the ball went sideways. Tore up my gun and hit you at the same time. I…." His voice breaks. "I never meant to harm you, I swear."

"It was just a mishap. I know that, and I forgive you."

He swallows hard, still shaking. "Thank you, Mistress. Is there anything I can do to help?"

"Mr. Fletcher, please, go find some of the Wampanoag people. Tell them I'm hurt, and please bring back Tekoa and Kesuk."

He nods. "I'll retrieve them."

Henry stands. "I'll accompany you."

They leave, and I hear the door close behind them and try to focus on staying conscious. Danielle presses a cool cloth to my forehead. Isaac's hand holds mine tight, warm against my clammy skin. I sip the water Danielle brings me, but the fever continues to gnaw away.

Danielle sighs. "I think it's you who's supposed to go back, Alyssa. You need medical attention, not me."

I let out a shaky laugh, wincing against the pain. "You're going to need medical attention when you have your baby."

She shakes her head, her voice firm but gentle. "No. People have had babies without doctors for thousands of years. I'm going to be fine. When I have all of my babies, I'm going to be fine."

I close my eyes, exhausted. "I... I think I'm supposed to stay in this time," I whisper. "And you're supposed to go home."

She smiles, squeezing my hand. "Maybe you're right," she says. "Maybe you're supposed to be here, but for now, just stay with me. Stay alive."

My head spins. Pain and fever blur the edges of the room. Everything turns black.

I WAKE TO THE ROAR OF RAIN AGAINST THE WINDOWS, WIND RATTLING the shutters, and the low rumble of thunder. My arm pulses, sharp and unrelenting, and the fever burns through me, making my head spin. I open my eyes, try to focus, and see Tekoa and Kesuk standing nearby, their faces grave.

"It's time to go," Tekoa says.

I frown, weak and confused. "Go where?"

Danielle slides onto the bed beside me, pressing a cool hand to my fevered forehead. "Alyssa, Kesuk says the great spirits are sending you back to our time."

Isaac sits close, his face pale with worry, his eyes fixed on me.

I look at him, my heart hammering. "I don't want to leave you."

"I don't want you to leave either, but you need to go where they can save your life," he says, his voice quiet but certain.

Danielle leans closer, her eyes gleaming despite her worry. "Do you remember when we were in junior high, and we found those neat rocks in the cave? Remember where that was?"

I try to think through the haze, then a faint, bittersweet smile tugs at my lips. "Of course. Not too far from here, actually. At the bonfire on my grandfather's land, in the mouth of the cave. You and I snuck into the cave, and they were just lying there."

She smiles softly. "When you get back to 2025, you'll go there. Dig down into the ground right at that spot. There will be a chest. I'll write you a letter every single day for the rest of my life, so you'll know how it all turned out."

Reality hits me like a truck. I'm leaving my best friend since kindergarten in the seventeenth century. I'm going back alone and wounded. My stomach twists, fever and grief mixing.

Kesuk lifts her hands, chanting low and solemn in Wôpanâak. Tekoa translates: "Let the river of time open her mouth. Let the winding roads remember every name. One walks forward, one remains behind."

I hear voices outside singing a chant in unison.

"The tribe has called the storm. The spirits have answered. It is time to go home," Tekoa says.

Tears burn my eyes. I turn to Danielle, clutching her shoulders, memorizing her warmth, the sound of her voice, and the feel of her hair against my skin. "I don't want to leave you," I whisper, my voice cracking.

"I don't want you to either, but you have to. I love you. I'll love you forever."

"I'll love you forever, too." I press my forehead to hers, my breath ragged. "Goodbye, Danielle."

She grips me one last time, whispering, "Goodbye, Alyssa."

Isaac lifts me carefully from the bed. My head falls against his chest, fever blurring my every thought. The wind howls outside. The door creaks open, and rain slashes through the air in sheets. Tekoa and Kesuk step out first, their voices joining the storm, carrying the chant.

The yard is crowded. Villagers stand in the rain, their faces pale in the lightning. Samoset and Tisquantum are here, Massasoit Ousamequin beside them, their eyes lifted to the sky, their voices rising in rhythm.

Isaac carries me through the doorway, the downpour soaking us. The fever has me half-delirious, but I can still feel the way he clutches me, as if letting go will break him.

His voice is low, unsteady. "I don't want to lose you," he says, rain streaming down his face. "I'll miss you every day, Alyssa. I'll never take another wife. I'll stay here, and I'll pray for you for the rest of my life. I love you."

My throat tightens. "I love you, too," I whisper. "I don't want to go without you."

He stares into my eyes for a moment and kisses my forehead, grief breaking through his composure. Lightning flashes, white and blinding. The chant grows louder, echoing across the village as Kesuk raises her hands to the sky. I can barely hold my eyes open now.

Everything rises into the roar of the storm as the chant crescendos, thunder cracks, and the world dissolves into rain and light.

IS SHE ALIVE?

THE RAIN IS RELENTLESS, BUT ALL I CAN SEE IS ALYSSA, PALE AND trembling. Her head is pressed against my chest as I carry her down through the sand toward the shore. The waves crash against the rocks.

Tisquantum and Samoset are there already, their muscles straining as they steady a small rowboat at the water's edge. The storm howls around them, and lightning claws across the black sky. Kesuk stands in the shallows, her silver hair whipping around her like smoke, chanting in that strange, ancient rhythm that makes the air itself feel alive.

Tekoa points to the boat. "Go!" she cries. "Go with her!"

I don't hesitate. I wade forward, the surf dragging at my legs, and lift Alyssa higher against me.

Her eyes flutter open, dazed. "Isaac…."

"I'm here," I whisper, though my voice is lost to the gale.

Samoset steadies the boat as I climb in, still holding Alyssa close.

The moment we push off, the sea takes us, tossing, spinning, alive with fury. I look back once, through the sheets of rain, to see Tekoa and the others still chanting on the shore.

The current pulls us faster, farther from land. The wind screams, and the sky flashes with light. Alyssa stirs weakly, her breath shallow against my neck.

I press my forehead to hers, desperate to memorize her warmth. "Stay with me," I beg. "Just a little longer."

The boat lurches, the bow rising high on a wave then crashing down hard. Water floods the bottom, cold as death. I try to bail it out with my free hand, but another wave slams into us. The rope snaps. The oars fly from their locks. The sea roars louder than the thunder.

The next wave hits harder than any before. The boat lifts, turns, and for a split second, we're suspended in air before crashing sideways into the churning black water.

The cold steals my breath. Salt burns my throat. I'm dragged under, still clutching her. My eyes sting open to darkness, foam, and flashes of light from the storm above. She's limp in my arms, her hair floating around us.

I kick upward, my lungs screaming. We break the surface for a moment, long enough for me to gasp her name. "Alyssa!"

Lightning explodes across the sky. The thunder cracks so loud it feels like the world itself is splitting apart. Then another wave swallows us whole. I hold her tighter, refusing to let go, even as the current pulls us down into the endless dark.

And then cold–cold is all I feel at first. I close my eyes and sink for what seems like hours. We are pulled through a cavern of darkness. I can't breathe, and I feel weak.

My eyes sting when I force them open again. Alyssa is still in my arms, her head against my shoulder.

I tighten my grip and kick toward the light. My muscles scream. I break the surface and drag in a desperate breath. Waves crash around us, but the storm is gone, replaced by sunlight.

People dot the beach—unfamiliar people. Some of them shout and run into the water.

Many of the men wear hats and cloaks like mine; others are dressed like the Wampanoag, but more are in colors and fabrics I've never seen: shiny, smooth, too bright for the world I know.

"Alyssa!" I gasp, choking on seawater. I try to keep her head above the waves. Two men in strange yellow coats rush toward us. One of them shouts, "We've got them! Get the stretcher!"

I don't know what that word means, but before I can ask, they haul us both from the surf. My knees buckle.

There's a noise like thunder, constant and mechanical, and I look up to see a massive metal beast with flashing red and blue lights rolling toward us. It's unlike any wagon I've ever seen, moving without horses, roaring with life.

They lift Alyssa first, strapping her onto a narrow bed that slides into the back of the contraption. "Sir, we'll take care of you. We've got you both."

"We're together," I manage to say. "She's hurt. Her shoulder, please—"

"We know," a woman answers, her face kind but hurried. "You and your wife are going to the hospital."

I climb in after Alyssa, and the beastly machine jolts forward. I sit on a bench, clutching it on either side, the motion incredibly fast, strange, and terrifying. The machine makes a loud, uncomfortable noise the entire time it travels, and when we reach our destination, people surround me. The smell here is sharp and unnatural. Hands press against my arms, checking my scrapes, my bruises. Someone wraps my wrist in white cloth that sticks to itself.

"Can you tell us your name?" a nurse asks.

"Isaac Owens," I say automatically.

"And where are you from?"

I hesitate, my eyes darting around the gleaming room. Glass, metal, lights—nothing here belongs to my world. "From here," I say carefully.

She smiles. "Right, part of the festival, then, the Pilgrim reenactment? We figured that's what all the costumes were for."

I nod, playing along because it's easier than the truth. I suddenly realize what Alyssa and Danielle must've gone through when they had to lie to Henry and me that first day on the shore.

Another woman dressed in white enters. "They found your car in the harbor. You and your wife are lucky to be alive."

My heart leaps. "Is she alive?"

"Yes," the nurse says gently. "She's alive. She's in surgery now."

Relief crashes through me, and I whisper her name. All I can do is pray that she recovers.

After a while, they move her into the room. She's pale and still, her shoulder wrapped in bandages. The steady sound of a machine keeps time, and I can hardly breathe until I see her chest rise and fall.

"She made it through surgery," a woman tells me softly. "We repaired all the damage. She'll wake soon."

When they leave, I pull my chair closer to her bed and reach for her hand, whispering, "You're safe, Alyssa. You're home."

She opens her eyes groggy, smiling faintly. "Home," she repeats, her voice rough. "I can't believe it."

I nod, though my throat is too tight for words. She looks up at the ceiling, tears shining at the corners of her eyes. "I can't wait to call my parents," she whispers. "To see them again. To tell them everything."

Her laugh is weak, breathless, but it's the most beautiful sound I've ever heard. She turns her head toward me, her eyes bright despite the exhaustion. "I'm so glad you came with me, Isaac. I didn't think it was possible."

I stand, leaning over her, brushing a damp strand of hair from her forehead. "There's nowhere else I'd rather be," I tell her, and I press my lips to her cheek.

Sinking into the chair beside her, I'm still dizzy from the impossible—being thrust four hundred years ahead, facing a world I don't recognize, and feeling helpless while she was in surgery. Alas, she's here, awake and breathing. Somehow, I'm with her, and that's all that matters.

For the first time since she was shot, my chest unclenches, and I let myself feel the wild relief of simply being with her.

HOME

Alyssa

I wake up groggy from surgery, glad to see I'm in a private room. Blinking my eyes open, I see Isaac sitting next to me, wearing what must be clothes the hospital provided—ill-fitting sweats. He smiles and takes my hand. "How are you?"

"Tired," I mange, but I also smile. He must be terrified to be here. "What day is it?"

"The day after Thanksgiving," he whispers. "You were only gone a short time. The rest of the day, you were in surgery and resting."

My mouth drops open. All those months spent in the past were only moments here.

When the nurses come and check on my IV and ask me if I need anything after surgery, the only thing I can think of is my family.

As if reading my mind, the nurse says, "Your family is waiting to see you. Shall I let them in?"

I nod, and only a moment passes before the door bursts open, and my mother's voice fills the room. "Oh, thank God!" She rushes to my side, her hands carefully framing my face as she inspects me. My dad is right behind her, his eyes full of relief, while James and Chloe hover at the foot of my bed.

"You scared us half to death," Chloe says, trying to laugh.

"I'm okay," I promise, even though my throat feels tight. "It looks worse than it is."

"What happened?" Dad asks.

I glance at Isaac beside me, and my family seems to notice him for the first time. "A bullet from the woods hit my shoulder, and I lost control of the car. A hunter must have accidentally shot at the road, I guess. We went off the road and into the water." The lie tastes strange on my tongue, but it's the only version of the truth they can believe. "Isaac here pulled me out. If it weren't for him…."

Mom's gaze follows mine to him. "Yes, we met earlier," she says with a fond smile. "Thank you again for saving our daughter."

Isaac smiles. "I did what anyone would've done. I'm just glad Alyssa is okay." His voice is soft and kind, and my heart twists at how out of place he looks surrounded by electric machines and fluorescent light. I make a quick explanation to my family members of this man I love, who has to pretend to be practically a stranger, at least for a while. They seem to believe that Isaac and I met before the feast, and he just happened by when the accident occurred and was able to jump in and save me.

Dad moves to shake his hand. "Well, you're a hero in my book."

"Thank you, sir."

Mom fusses over me again, shifting my blanket even though it doesn't need adjusting. James keeps glancing at Isaac like he's trying to figure out who he is and where he came from. I can't answer that question right now and sound even half sane, so I just breathe and take in the moment. I'm finally home with my family.

And then it hits me, the silence where Danielle's loud laugh should be, and my heart sinks.

"There's something else," I manage. "Danielle was with me."

Chloe's head snaps up. "Where is she? Is she okay?"

I stare at my hands. "I don't know. They can't find her."

The words hang heavy in the room. Mom presses her hand to her mouth. Dad lowers his head. Even James turns away. Chloe sits down in a chair and sobs. My parents murmur about going to help with the search, but they ultimately determine to spend some time with me first and let the emergency workers do their job.

Conversation is light, centered mostly about how I'm feeling now, not how it was in those moments of terror revolving around the accident. The machines keep their rhythm, steady and cruel, as if the world hasn't just split in two.

When my family leaves the hospital to allow me to rest, they say they'll plan a search for Danielle and that they'll be back to see me in the morning. I am so grateful to be back with them, and I love them more than I can put into words. I make a silent vow to myself and Danielle to spend every second of the rest of my life appreciating and loving the people around me.

A few days pass in a haze of antiseptic, soft voices, and the slow rhythm of recovery. My shoulder heals better than I expect, the stitches neat beneath the bandage. Isaac stays in my room as much as he can until they finally release me. The doctors call me "lucky." I know it's something deeper than luck.

For days, authorities search for Danielle. But of course, they never find her. Before I'm even dismissed from the hospital, she's presumed dead.

My father drives the minivan, with my mother in the front, and I sit in the back with Isaac, my siblings in the way-back. No one has questioned why Isaac and I are inseparable, and I'm glad for it. As we drive, I think about all the changes coming my way. A new car, a new roommate in Isaac, everything he'll need in order to acclimate to our world. It's a lot, but we'll take it one step at a time.

The first place we go isn't home. It's the park by the harbor, where a memorial is being held for Danielle. Candles glow in the cool evening air, their light trembling across rows of faces. Everyone's bundled in coats, holding small white roses. Chloe printed a photo of my best friend, one from college, where her hair's wild from the wind, and she's laughing at something I said. I can't breathe when I see it.

People take turns speaking. They talk about how bright she was, how funny and kind. No one knows that four centuries ago, she carried a child, that she spent her days smiling at Henry by a fire in a version of Plymouth that hasn't existed for hundreds of years. To everyone here, her life was cut short. They'll never know the happiness she truly experienced, and it hurts my heart that I can't tell them.

Isaac stands beside me, his expression unreadable but his hand warm around mine. I can feel his grief as much as my own. He's lost so much, too.

When it's my turn to step forward, I can barely speak. "Danielle was my best friend," I manage, my voice breaking. "She was brave, impossibly selfless, and she loved harder than anyone I've ever known." I pause, swallowing hard.

A tear slips down my cheek, and Isaac squeezes my hand. The candles blur through my tears, and for a heartbeat, I swear I see her, standing in the glow, smiling, the wind tugging at her hair like it is in the picture.

Then, she's gone.

When her father steps up to speak after me, her mother at his side, I am thankful that they at least showed up to this. Their tears make me wonder what might've been if they'd shown her the love she deserved before we slipped back through time.

After the vigil, we walk back to the van in silence, the air heavy with sadness, salt, and smoke. The sea stretches dark and endless behind us.

At my house, everything feels so modern and bright. The heat hums through the vents, the lights come on with a switch, and Isaac looks at his surroundings as if my home is full of magic.

I brew tea while he studies a photo on the mantle of Danielle and me on the beach last summer, our arms around each other, both smiling at the camera. He glances at me. "She was always so happy," he says quietly. "No matter what."

"She was." My voice catches. "And I think she still is."

He nods, the only person alive not questioning what that means.

I sit beside him on the couch, and for the first time since we came back, it's quiet. The world feels strange and too fast, but he's here, solid, real, and warm beside me.

After a while, he teases, "Do you still want to marry me?"

I tilt my head, smiling up at him. "Of course I do. Also, you have no idea how incredibly sexy you look in these new clothes," I whisper. "You're unfairly handsome."

His cheeks flush, that familiar shy smile playing at his lips. "Unfairly?"

"Yes, it's unfair to all the other men of this time. You're so ridiculously hot."

He leans down and kisses me. When we stretch out together, his arms still wrapped around me, I feel completely safe. I fall asleep there beside him, loved and certain that this is exactly where I'm meant to be–here and now... with him.

By morning, life is feeling a bit more normal. The sky is deep blue outside my kitchen window, and sunlight pours across the table where Isaac sits, awkwardly but curiously eating a bowl of cereal.

As I butter toast, a thought sparks. I look up at Isaac. "Do you remember what Danielle told us about the cave on my grandfather's land?"

He nods slowly. "A place she wanted us to find."

"Let's go find it!" I say, dropping the toast and picking up the keys to a rental car my parents took care of for me.

An hour later, after grabbing a shovel from the hardware store, we're driving down the old coastal road, the wind roaring through the cracked windows. I know this road by heart. The cliff side is overgrown, but I recognize the slope of the land, the jagged rocks, the curve of the inlet.

We climb down the narrow path until we find the cave's mouth, half-hidden by vines and dirt. The air is cool and damp inside. Isaac digs until he hits something solid, and my heart jumps.

We clear away the rest of the dirt, and there is a large chest, weathered but intact, the iron hinges streaked with rust but still holding. The initials carved into the lid are faint but unmistakable: D.W.L.

"Danielle Whitman-Lewis," I gasp.

Isaac and I lift it together. It's heavier than I expect. We load it carefully into the car, fill in the hole, and drive home.

At my house, Isaac sets the chest on a sheet I've spread out on the living room floor. The latch creaks as I open it. Inside are bundles of letters tied with ribbon, small hand-sewn baby clothes, and sketches. The scent of time itself seems to rise from the old ink, linen, and memories.

I unfold the first letter. Henry's handwriting is rough but steady.

To my friend Isaac, who taught me that courage is not the absence of fear but the choice to keep going despite it.

I can't read the rest aloud. My throat clenches, tears burning behind my eyes.

There are letters from the Connor children, written in careful script, telling of harvests, marriages, and new babies. Danielle's handwriting appears again and again, and I can hear her beautiful voice across the centuries. One letter reads, We have lived a long, full life. We never forgot you. I hope you are with your family and Isaac; happy, whole, and loved.

At the very bottom lies a thick stack of pages, neatly bound. The first line makes me hold my breath in awe.

The guides Samoset and Squanto were more than just guides to the pilgrims. They guided a time traveler named Alyssa, who walked between centuries and helped save a colony that was never meant to survive without her. A story by Danielle "Big Fan" Whitman-Lewis.

"This is a manuscript. Danielle wrote a book about us!"

Isaac and I look at each other through tears.

"She told our story," I whisper. "She wrote it all down."

He nods, his voice rough. "Then, we should finish what she started."

I smooth a hand over the cover, the paper fragile beneath my fingertips. "We'll publish it," I say. "The world should know who they were and about our lives back then, even if they think it's all make believe."

The chest sits open between us, full of the lives we left behind. Somehow, it feels less like we left our friends in the past and more like they've finally come home.

WHEN THE TIME IS RIGHT

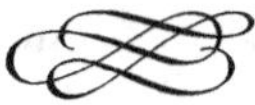

THE SUN IS ALREADY UP WHEN I PULL THE TRUCK INTO THE SCHOOL parking lot to drop Alyssa off. Her golden hair shines in the morning light, and she's laughing because I still turn the windshield wipers on when I mean to use the blinker. I can't help it. There are too many levers and too many lights.

She leans over, kisses my cheek, and says, "You're getting better, Ranger Owens." Then she's out of the truck and striding toward the school doors. Every bit of her fits in this world that I'm still learning.

It's been a month, and I'm still trying to understand how everything works. People move quickly here. They talk faster and use words I don't understand. They eat food that comes in boxes and drink water from plastic bottles instead of wells. There are machines for everything: washing clothes, cleaning dishes, and even talking. There's even a voice in my phone that tells me where to go. The first time I heard a voice from the phone telling me to "turn left," I nearly threw it out the window. Alyssa just laughed until she cried.

Now, I spend my mornings on job sites, working as a carpenter.

My boss says I've got a "good eye for detail," which makes me proud. I like the smell of sawdust. It's one of the few things that feels the same no matter what century I'm in. Wood still speaks the same language. I measure, cut, and shape it until it fits just right. There's something beautiful in that, and it keeps me from getting overwhelmed. Alyssa managed to get me the paperwork I needed in a way I didn't understand. Now, I was born in 1995 instead of 1595. How odd.

In the evenings, I go to class at the local college. Eventually, I want to work as a park ranger, working outside again and protecting the forests instead of cutting them down.

When I come home in the evenings, Alyssa's usually cooking something that fills the house with warmth. We eat together at the little table in our kitchen. Often, we talk about Danielle and Henry.

I never imagined I'd live like this—with light switches that chase away the dark, music that comes from a box the size of my hand, or a truck that can carry us anywhere in minutes, but it's not the truck, the house or the lights that make this life worthwhile.

It's her.

Every morning when I wake up beside her, I remember the sound of waves and the storm that brought us here—the fear, the cold, and the way she held on to me even when everything else was lost. That memory makes every strange part of this world seem small.

Sometimes, when the day is done, we drive out to her grandfather's land. We park under the stars and sit in the bed of the truck. She leans against me, and I'm reminded that it doesn't matter what year it is. I'm four centuries from home, but I don't miss the past.

My home is with Alyssa.

Alyssa

I sit at the kitchen table. The house is quiet except for the low hum of the coffeemaker and the occasional car outside. Isaac leans against the counter, his sleeves rolled up from a morning of projects. He's so cute when he's busy with something he's passionate about.

There's a calmness here, a kind of normal I never thought I'd feel again after enduring the seventeenth century and losing Danielle.

Teaching keeps me busy, but sometimes the ache of her absence creeps in like an unwelcome shadow. I miss her every day, even though the classroom is bright and chaotic, a stark reminder that life goes on, even when part of my heart is frozen in another time.

Holding Danielle's words in my hands and reading the story from her perspective made her feel close again. Her courage, humor, and brilliance, was captured for everyone to read. Publishing her manuscript was both healing and terrifying.

Isaac pulls out a chair beside me, sliding in with a casual ease. I feel safe and loved in the little things. Now, it's just the two of us, navigating a future we never expected, together.

"We should pick a date soon," I say, more to myself than him. Planning the wedding feels strange, surreal even, but also exhilarating. Every time I think about walking down the aisle toward Isaac, the man who once followed me through a storm four hundred years into the future, my heart speeds up.

He nods, his eyes reflecting a quiet satisfaction. "I'm ready when you're ready," he says. His words are simple, but they carry patience, love, and devotion.

I glance out the window, imagining our life together: mornings filled with sunlight, our laughter echoing in this little house, the scent of Isaac's woodworking projects mingling with my coffee. The quiet evenings, the new adventures we'll go on, and the knowledge that, no matter what, we are building this life together from scratch. Every step we take is ours to claim.

"Do you ever think we'll have a baby?" I ask softly, almost afraid to voice it aloud.

He looks at me, beaming. "Of course! I want to have lots of babies with you." He slides the chair closer and wraps his arms around me, squeezing gently. "When the time is right, we'll figure it out together. You'll be the most incredible mother, Alyssa."

Joy blooms in my chest as I picture tiny feet slapping these floors, laughter pouring through the kitchen, little hands reaching for cookies. The thought feels new and exciting, like another piece of the life we're building is finally coming into focus. I know for certain, if we have a little girl, her name will be Danielle. Our first son will be named Henry.

We sit in quiet companionship for a moment, his arms around me, imagining what the future might hold. The purest joy isn't found in just the wedding, the house, or even the work we do. It's the life we'll share, the family we might create, the miraculously ordinary days that will be ours.

I think of Danielle and Henry, of the lives they lived, the family they raised, the love they nurtured, and I smile, bittersweet but hopeful. They existed. They thrived. They were happy, and through Danielle's book, through every memory and keepsake, we can hold them close.

I watch our lives unfolding, the small good that we do and the love we build, hoping it leaves a mark. Maybe, four hundred years from now, someone will read about us and know we were here, that we mattered, and that we tried to make our time meaningful.

Thank you for reading! Book 9, Back to Whitechapel, *will be out December 15, 2025. If you love romantic suspense, you'll love this Jack the Ripper inspired tale!*

ALSO BY ID JOHNSON

Stand Alone Titles

<u>All I Want for Christmas is Pooch</u>

(*sweet contemporary romance*)

<u>Christmas Memory</u>

(*sweet contemporary romance*)

<u>Meet Cute Me Under the Mistletoe</u>

(*sweet contemporary romance*)

<u>The Doll Maker's Daughter at Christmas</u>

(*clean romance/historical*)

<u>Pretty Little Monster</u>

(*young adult/suspense*)

<u>The Journey to Normal: Our Family's Life with Autism</u> (*nonfiction*)

<u>Found by the Alpha (*fantasy romance*)</u>

Sweet As Maple Syrup series

Leaving Autumn

Cold Turkey

Snowed Inn (coming Dec 1, 2025!)

Love Throughout Time

(*time travel romance*)

Back to Titanic (free!)

Back to Gettysburg

Back to Bunker Hill

Back to the Highlands

Back to Port Royal

Back to the Inquisition

Back to Salem

Back to Plymouth

Back to Whitechapel (Dec 2025)

Back to the Old West (Jan 2026)

Back to the Ton (Feb 2026)

Back to the Crown (March 2026)

Back to Pompeii (April 2026)

Silverwood Academy

(paranormal romance)

Vampire Hunter (free!)

World Builder

Realm Jumper

Celestial Springs

(psychological thriller/literary fiction/women's fiction)

Beneath the Inconstant Moon

The First Mrs. Edwards

Leaving Ginny

The Motherhood

(dystopian romance)

Rain's Rebellion (free!)

Rain's Run

Rain's Return

Ashes and Rose Petals

(contemporary romance/retelling of Romeo and Juliet and Cinderella)

Girl in the Attic (free!)

Girl From the Tomb

<u>Girl On the Beach</u>

Nashville Country Dreams

(contemporary romance)

<u>Meant to Marry Me (free!)</u>

<u>Lead Me Home</u>

<u>You Are the Reason</u>

Forever Love series

(clean romance/historical)

<u>Cordia's Will: A Civil War Story of Love and Loss</u>

<u>Cordia's Hope: A Story of Love on the Frontier</u>

The Clandestine Saga series

(paranormal romance)

<u>Transformation (free!)</u>

<u>Resurrection</u>

<u>Repercussion</u>

<u>Absolution</u>

<u>Illumination</u>

<u>Destruction</u>

<u>Annihilation</u>

<u>Obliteration</u>

<u>Termination</u>

A Vampire Hunter's Tale (based on The Clandestine Saga)

(paranormal/alternate history)

<u>Aaron (free!)</u>

<u>Jamie</u>

<u>Elliott</u>

<u>Christian</u>

The Chronicles of Cassidy (based on The Clandestine Saga)

(young adult paranormal)

So You Think Your Sister's a Vampire Hunter? (free!)

Who Wants to Be a Vampire Hunter?

How Not to Be a Vampire Hunter

My Life As a Teenage Vampire Hunter

Vampire Hunting Isn't for Morons

Vampires Bite and Other Life Lessons

Gone Guardian

Death Does Not Become Her

Blood of the Vampire Hunter (based on The Clandestine Saga)

(paranormal romance)

Night Slayer (free!)

Shadow Stalker

Queen Catcher

Mother Hunter

Father Finder

Ghosts of Southampton series

(historical romance)

Prelude

Titanic

Residuum

Lusitania

Heartwarming Holidays Sweet Romance series

(Christian/clean romance)

Melody's Christmas (free!)

Christmas Cocoa

Winter Woods

Waiting On Love

Shamrock Hearts

A Blossoming Spring Romance

Firecracker!

Falling in Love

Thankful for You

Melody's Christmas Wedding

The New Year's Date

Charles Town Brides (based on Heartwarming Holidays Sweet Romance)

(Christian/clean romance)

From This Moment (free!)

Can't Help Falling in Love

It's Your Love

When You Say Nothing At All

My Girl

Unchained Melody

I Only Have Eyes For You

At Last

The Very Thought of You

Reaper's Hollow

(paranormal/urban fantasy)

Ruin's Lot (free!)

Ruin's Promise

Ruin's Legacy

When Kings Collide

(steamy historical romance)

Princess of Silence

<u>Princess of Hearts</u>

Collections

<u>Ghosts of Southampton Books 0-2</u>

<u>Reaper's Hollow Books 1-3</u>

<u>The Clandestine Saga Books 1-3</u>

<u>The Chronicles of Cassidy Books 1-4</u>

<u>Celestial Springs Collection</u>

<u>Heartwarming Holidays Sweet Romance Books 1-3</u>

<u>Heartwarming Holidays Sweet Romance Books 4-7</u>

Websites: https://idjohnsonwriter.com/

Follow us on TikTok: @roguewolfpublishing

Follow on Twitter @authoridjohnson

Find me on Facebook at <u>www.facebook.com/IDJohnsonAuthor</u>

Instagram: @authoridjohnson

Follow me on Bookbub: https://www.bookbub.com/authors/id-johnson